Ladies Night

Ladies Night

Christian Keyes

www.urbanbooks.net

Urban Books, LLC
97 N18th Street
Wyandanch, NY 11798

Ladies Night Copyright © 2014 Christian Keyes

ISBN 13: 978-1-62286-961-9
ISBN 10: 1-62286-961-3

First Mass Market Printing January 2016
First Trade Paperback Printing December 2014
Printed in the United States of America

10 9 8 7 6 5 4 3 2 1

This is a work of fiction. Any references or similarities to actual events, real people, living or dead, or to real locales are intended to give the novel a sense of reality. Any similarity in other names, characters, places, and incidents is entirely coincidental.

Distributed by Kensington Publishing Corp.
Submit Orders to:
Customer Service
400 Hahn Road
Westminster, MD 21157-4627
Phone: 1-800-733-3000
Fax: 1-800-659-2436

What People Are Saying About *Ladies Night*

"If this story were any hotter, the book would catch fire. *Ladies Night* is a smart and sexy page-turner."

—Vivica A. Fox

"I couldn't put the book down. It was an exciting and sexy ride, and I enjoyed every minute of it!"

—Jackie Christie, *Basketball Wives LA*

"There hasn't been a book this sexy with a purpose since Michael Baisden's *Maintenance Man* and Carl Weber's *The Man in 3B*."

—N.D. Brown, CEO Tri Destined Studios

Dedication

I dedicate this book to the supporters and fans who have had my back for years. It is because of your support that I am able to do what I do. Thank you!!!

Acknowledgments

I want to thank the people who helped make this happen: Carl Weber, Joylynn M. Ross, and N.D. Brown. I thank God for the blessing of having a book publishing deal. I know how much of a blessing it is to have a company believe in you and how hard it is to get a deal, let alone write the book, so thank you!

Lastly, I want thank John Jablonski, the extremely strict critical-writing teacher I had in college. The way you taught us how to research, outline, and build a research paper just clicked. You telling me to consider changing my curriculum to critical-writing really gave me confidence in my writing, because you were arguably the toughest S.O.B. to get a good grade from at the school. You're probably going to grade and make notes on this acknowledgments page, lol. Either way, thank you!

Chapter 1

The gate slammed loudly behind Amp Anthony, but he didn't flinch, in spite of the fact that the sound took him back to the first time he'd heard it. Years had passed since then, but he remembered it like it was just yesterday. That sound had been a prelude to the harsh reality that he would no longer be a free man for quite some time. Now, that same sound announced his return to the free world.

As Amp walked past, the portly little corrections officer sneered at him. "See you around."

Without looking back, Amp announced with conviction, "No, you won't." He threw his worn out duffle bag over his shoulder and walked through the outer gate, pausing for a second to consider taking one last look at the prison that had been his home for the last four and a half years.

With the afternoon sun illuminating the sign that read CALIFORNIA STATE PENITENTIARY, Amp decided not to turn around. He wouldn't look back—not at the prison, and damn sure not at that life. Although almost every inmate who had ever been lucky enough to make it this far outside of those painted cement walls had probably vowed the same, Amp was determined to follow through. He'd made up his mind that whatever he had to do to stay on the straight and narrow, it was as good as done. His past was behind him.

The last five years had been hell for the now twenty-nine-year-old felon, but black don't crack. So, even though the time served had been rough on him mentally, it hadn't taken a toll on his appearance. In fact, he was stronger. Aside from reading as a mental escape, Amp had spent his time lifting weights and playing ball, which resulted in him adding twenty pounds of pure, cut muscle. Standing six feet three inches tall, weighing 205 pounds with a size 13 boot, he was definitely all man.

Amp was ruggedly handsome, even if a little rough around the edges. He had a visible and ungroomed beard, and it had nothing to do with the fad that seemed to be sweeping the NBA. For the most part he had tried to keep a nice edge up, but he still wore his ever-present signature black skull cap. He had caramel skin, big brown eyes, thick eyebrows, and the kind of eyelashes that piss women off.

In his faded, state-issued blue jeans and matching jean jacket, Amp had a mean swagger about himself, a quiet confidence. It wasn't something he tried to do, and that made him stand out even more. There was a look of focus in his eyes, but if you looked closely, you would also see guilt, shame, and regret lurking there. It was obvious that he had been through a lot in his life.

Outside the prison gates, Amp spotted a black man, who appeared to be a few years older than him, leaning on an old white Ford. Amp wondered who life had been the toughest for: the man or his beat-up looking car. It was apparent he was waiting on someone, considering there were a million and one other places he could have been besides standing outside a prison facility with the sun baking his dark brown skin. Since Amp was being released from jail to a halfway house, he had an idea of who this gentleman might be.

"You Amp Anthony?" the man asked.

Amp looked him up and down, trying to read what type of cat he'd be dealing with. "Yeah." His response was short.

The man walked over to Amp with an extended hand. "I'm Paul Harold."

Amp raised his hand to block the sun and squinted his eyes to get a better look at the

modestly dressed man, who was wearing a pair
of khakis and a plaid button-up with some black
laced dress shoes. Upon closer inspection, the
man looked to be about forty years old. Even
though he had a few years on Amp, his thick
arms bulging through his sleeves looked as
though they were no stranger to pumping a little
iron. He wasn't as muscular or defined as Amp,
but clearly he could hold his own.

Amp looked at the man's extended hand for
a moment. Still trying to read this guy, he hesitated, uncertain whether he wanted to come
off as a hard ass or as a likeable guy. He had
learned quickly in the joint that he couldn't treat
everybody the same. Although Amp had been
raised by parents who taught him to treat others
with respect, life had shown him that there was a
price to pay for being too nice. Cats would sometimes get it twisted and take Amp's kindness for
weakness, and that only led to drama.

One time in particular, not long after he had
entered the joint, an inmate asked Amp if he
could have a portion of his meal. Amp hadn't
planned on eating anyway; prison food took
some getting used to, and Amp hadn't accom-
plished that task just yet. So, Amp didn't think
twice about handing it over to the guy. This
happened a couple of times, causing the guy to

catch a case of entitlement. When Amp declined one day to give him any portion of his meal, dude tried to test Amp by taking it and pushing him down. Unfortunately for the inmate, Amp smashed his teeth in with the tray and beat the hell out of him. Amp was placed in solitary confinement. The upside was that afterward, guys left Amp alone.

This Paul character didn't look like he was about the drama, which was why Amp chose the likable-guy route and shook his hand.

"I run the halfway house you'll be calling home for the next ninety days," Paul said.

Amp nodded, signaling his understanding. Another thing he'd acquired in the pen was discretion. Once guys figured out he was handy with a pair of clippers, they came to Amp for haircuts. He discovered he could learn twice as much from listening as he could from talking, which is probably why God gave man two ears and only one mouth. He'd also learned to speak only when he had something to say. Life was too short to be wasted on useless words when actions were louder anyway.

Paul continued. "Toss your bag in the back." He nodded over his shoulder toward the white Ford. "I'll explain the rules of the house on the way there." Pulling his keys out of his pocket, Paul popped the trunk then got into the driver's seat.

Amp put his bag in the trunk of the state-issued vehicle, slammed it shut, and then got into the car.

"Damn, you think you closed the trunk hard enough?" Paul asked sarcastically.

"Just making sure it's closed. That's my whole life back there in that bag . . . or what's left of it."

Paul simply looked ahead and started the car. He pulled off of the gravel-covered lot, leaving dust behind.

"I'm strict but fair," Paul started as Amp quietly observed the scenery passing by. Everything appeared to be more vibrant than he remembered.

Amp cracked the window. Now that he was free, he didn't like the idea of the glass separating him from the outside. The wind carried the aroma of independence to Amp's nose, and he inhaled deeply. No words could do justice to describe the sweet smell of his long-awaited liberty.

"Ninety days from now, if you make it through that time without incident, you will be a free man," Paul said.

Although Amp's focus remained on the trees, the road, the wind, things that free men took for granted on a daily basis, he listened intently to Paul's words. The last thing he wanted to do was screw up, landing his ass back in prison with only memories of all he was taking in right now.

"While you're at the house, no company, no drugs, no drinking, no fighting, no partying, no stealing, no missing curfew, no fuck-ups of any kind," Paul rattled off.

"That's an awful lot of no's," Amp said, turning to look at Paul.

Paul shot him a stern look. "I can swing a U-turn, take your black ass back to the joint, and you can spend your last ninety days in that cage if my rules sound like too much for you."

Amp's mind flashed to the still-fresh images of being caged up, being told what he could and couldn't do and when he could and couldn't do it twenty-four hours a day. "Nah. Continue."

With his eyes back on the road, Paul continued running down his list of expectations. "Don't think you're going to just be sitting around the house catching up on reality TV," Paul said firmly. "You are required to either get a job or enroll in classes within a short but reasonable time after your arrival. You can do both if you want to. It may help the time go faster."

Amp let a chuckle make its way through his teeth. "You think somebody's gonna be in a rush to hire someone with my record?"

Paul didn't answer. He just shook his head and twisted up the right corner of his mouth.

"What?" Amp asked.

"Already making excuses." He exhaled. "I can see exactly how this is going to go."

"Man, I ain't making no excuses. I'm making sense and you know it," Amp said, looking back out the window, trying to keep calm—and if nothing else, the sound, look, feel, smell, even the taste of nature, was indeed calming.

"Then prove yourself right," Paul said as he stopped at a light. "You gotta still go out there and at least try, not just to prove me wrong, but to show the state that you are at least making an effort. While you're out there, make copies of all the applications you turn in. That way we can show your parole officer that you have actually been trying to secure employment. You do that and they'll stay off your back."

"What about you?" Amp asked. "Will that keep you off my back too?"

"Hey, I'm just doing my job." Paul shrugged.

"Hmmm, what else?" Paul said as he thought about any rules and expectations he might have failed to mention. He snapped his finger. "Oh, yeah. Respect the other people in the house and do not touch their stuff. Also, you will be subject to random drug tests and you will have weekly chores."

Amp inhaled wearily. It was a lot to take in, but he knew he had to do it. Besides, if he could handle four and a half years in the joint, then ninety days in a halfway house should be a piece of cake.

Now that Paul was done listing rules, Amp asked, "You mind?" His hand was already on the radio dial.

Paul nodded and Amp turned it on. It was set to a station that was playing pop contemporary music. Amp scrunched up his face.

Noticing the look on Amp's face, Paul said, "Don't judge me."

Amp cracked a smile and Paul grinned—the first sign that the tension might be lifting. Perhaps the ice had been broken, or was at least beginning to melt a little.

Even so, Amp was still a little confused about Paul. Earlier Paul had come across more laid back. Now, in the car, as he rattled off all the rules, he was coming across as a slight hard ass. Amp supposed it could have been a routine for Paul, as far as dealing with the housemates and running down the game to them, like how a stewardess has to give passengers the safety rules over and over again no matter how many times they've flown before. It just becomes sort of mechanical. Either way, Amp felt like the music was comforting, and he hurried to find a song they could both enjoy.

He turned the dial until he got to a station that was playing R & B music. "Toni Braxton still making music?" he asked.

"No. I mean, yeah, but that's her baby sister Tamar, I think," Paul replied.

Amp bobbed his head to the song playing. Looking down, he noticed a manila file folder stuffed between the seat and the console. He pulled it back and saw that his name was on the tab. "You read my file?" he asked, a hint of nervousness behind his tone.

"Yep," Paul replied as tension filled the car. "I had to get your background before I approved you to come to this house. But just so you know, there's no judgment here. We all got our shit— different shit, but we all got it nonetheless."

Amp looked out the window again and said nothing as Paul continued to drive. Lord knows Amp had beat himself up enough over the years; especially when it came to the loss of his parents, Martha and Allen Anthony. They weren't physically dead, but it sure felt like it.

Amp thought back to the relationship he had with his parents before he went to prison. He was always closer to his mother than his father. She was less demanding than he was, and she accepted Amp for who he was, flaws and all. His father always wanted Amp to be more.

Dad was a health fanatic and a well-known community pediatrician. Amp doing anything short of following in his father's footsteps was a disappointment to him. He cared more about how the family appeared to be doing than how they actually were. Still, the family had Sunday dinner together at least once a month, and his dad attended most of Amp's home games to show his support to his son—publicly, at least. Things went south when Amp decided he wanted to make his own choices about a career and announced he didn't want to be a doctor. Amp wanted to major in business and own his own barber shop one day.

It hurt when his father made him move out and cut him off financially, but Amp began carving out his own way. Amp and his dad had even started to grow closer right before Amp went to prison. When his conviction hit the local newspapers, his father couldn't get far enough away from Amp. He eventually even stopped letting his wife visit Amp or write to him in prison. Dr. Anthony felt he had to protect the family name, and that meant disowning his wayward son. This cut Amp deeply, and the wounds still hadn't healed. He doubted that they ever would.

In prison, Amp had to watch other inmates enjoy time with their loved ones while the only people he had in the world, his own flesh and blood, wouldn't even write him a letter. His heart got heavy every time he thought about how he missed them, but out of habit, he usually camouflaged it with anger, or he kept himself busy so he wouldn't have to think about it. Now, a commotion jolted Amp out of his thoughts.

"Damn it!" Paul shouted as he slammed on the brakes, tires screeching. "Get the hell out of the street!" he yelled at some kids illegally crossing the road on their bikes. "Damn kids." He shook his head and pulled off.

The sound of the screeching tires took Amp back to another dark place in his past. As he waited for his racing heartbeat to slow down, he could only agree with Paul's earlier statement: *"We all got our shit . . ."* Amp had been knee deep in his.

Chapter 2

Amp noticed that the closer they got to the city, the worse the neighborhoods started to look. This, of course, was nothing new to Amp. He had grown up on the South Side of Los Angles. He was from the hood, so living there wouldn't be a problem for him. He cracked a brief smile when they drove past his high school. It reminded him of the good old days, when he was young, having fun, and laughing until his face hurt.

If I could only go back there, he thought.

Slowly his smile disappeared as the laughter echoing in his head began to fade away. He felt his own judgment coming on. The heavy burden of guilt and shame took its usual place on his tension-filled back. He blinked hard and looked out the window, hoping to direct his focus onto something else. It worked, for now. Amp resumed people-watching.

The turns and corners were coming quicker now. Amp assumed they must be getting close to their destination.

The old Ford turned onto West Jefferson, slowed down, and made a right into the cemented driveway of a modest two-story house with well-kept landscaping. As a matter of fact, as Amp looked around he noticed that none of the neighboring yards were littered with toys, bikes, laundry, or any of the typical signs of a hood neighborhood. It was pretty quiet and peaceful.

"Well, this is it," Paul said as he got out of the car.

Amp got out, grabbed his bag, and followed him into the house, up the stairway, then into a small bedroom. Amp looked around at the room that wasn't much bigger than his jail cell had been. In spite of its size, he would gladly take this little room over that 11x6 cell where he had spent the last 1,600 nights. At least here he would have some privacy. No cellmates to worry about. The new spot where he would lay his head had four walls, and they weren't cement. Amp would take staring at these four walls with the faded light-blue paint job any day.

Paul walked over to the foot of the bed. He raised his arms as a sign to let Amp know that what he saw was all that he was getting. He began the mini tour.

"Closet." Paul pointed to a skinny wooden door. "Bathroom." The small bathroom was right behind where Paul stood. The door was open just enough for Amp to see that the walls were painted plain old white.

A closet *and* a private bathroom—now this was a true luxury indeed for Amp. Paul had pointed out a hallway bathroom on their way to his living quarters, and Amp had been almost sure he'd have to share a bathroom with his housemates. Considering the odor that had been emanating from that bathroom, this private one was an unexpected and much appreciated surprise.

"And of course, bed." Paul nodded.

Amp looked down at the bed. The tan-colored linens didn't look any better than the ones in his cell, but it would still be far more comfortable than where he'd laid his head the last few years. It had a real box spring and mattress set. In addition to that, it was a double size bed. Now maybe Amp could roll over comfortably in his sleep without fear of landing on the floor. And even if he did, at least now it would be a carpeted floor.

The carpet on which they stood probably was the most recent upgrade in the room. That new carpet scent still permeated the air, which Amp breathed in deeply to savor.

"All your hygiene supplies are in your bathroom," Paul told Amp. "It's just your basics to tide you over until you can buy your own stuff: toothpaste, deodorant, soap. The state is already covering your room and board and three meals a day. Don't think they're going to see to it that they wash your ass too," Paul said matter-of-factly. "And please make sure you do just that. This place ain't that big. If you stink, we smell it, so make sure you take care of yourself."

Amp walked over and sat down on the bed, his duffle bag hanging on his shoulder. He bounced on it a couple of times as if testing out a mattress in the store. He wasn't trying to be picky to see if it was to his liking; he was just enjoying the fact that after so many years, he'd finally be sleeping on a bed that had some type of give to it—a bounce back. The smallest pleasures in life now brought him joy.

"Curfew is at eleven p.m." Paul walked over to the only window in the room and raised the blind, providing a clear view of the front yard. "Same time as lights out. Eleven o'clock, no exceptions, unless we can verify that you're working third shift. Don't come at me with that 'I missed the bus,' or 'my ride didn't show up.' Like I said, no excuses. Period. So, if you plan on trying to play those kind of games, don't even bother unpacking."

Amp continued to eyeball the room while Paul talked. He heard Paul loud and clear, but was still checking out his new living quarters. There wasn't much to look at—just a bed, a dresser with a clock on it, a chair, and the curtain-less window Paul was standing by—but it was his own personal space, something he would never take for granted again.

"Dinner is at six-thirty, and breakfast is at seven in the morning. Lunch, everybody is pretty much on their own. The goal is not to be here during lunch hours, but out working." He gave Amp a knowing look then said, "I think that just about covers everything." Making his way across the room, he stopped in the doorway and asked, "You need anything?"

"A real meal and a shower," Amp replied.

Paul looked down at his watch. "I think we can handle that. It's still a couple hours until dinner yet, but there's plenty of food left over from last night's meal." He nodded toward the bathroom. "Wash your hands, come on down and make a plate."

As Amp stood up to head to the bathroom, Paul added, "Oh, yeah. Usually there's a five-minute time limit on the showers, but you can take your time tonight."

Amp watched Paul exit the room, then he gave the room one last sweep. "Ninety days," he muttered to himself. "Ninety days." He had waited for this day for a long time, and now that he was here with his entire future laid ahead of him, he wondered if he would make it. Would everything be all right? Did he have what it would take to survive—or maybe even thrive? Deep down in his soul he knew that everything would be okay, but fear of the unknown was beginning to creep into his head. He had to shake it off and lean on his faith.

Amp walked over to the window, placing his duffle bag down on the chair as he stared out over the yard. The reality was just starting to sink in that he was a free man and could walk out the door anytime he wanted—as long as he was back by eleven. There was a whole world waiting for him to make his unique contribution to it. Amp just had to believe again that he had a greater destiny than the one his choices had granted him thus far.

With a grumbling sound coming from his stomach, Amp was reminded of his need for a meal. He went into the bathroom and scoped it out before washing his hands. Sink, toilet, and shower: that was all a brother needed. That and whatever hot meal was waiting for him downstairs.

Amp returned to his room about an hour later, planning to turn in for the night. Last night's leftovers of baked pork chops, rice, green beans, and buttered bread had been plenty to satisfy him for the evening. All he wanted to do was take a nice, hot shower and lay it down.

Amp closed his bedroom door behind him. It creaked just a little, and he had to lift it slightly to get it to catch in the door plates. Realizing that there was no lock on the door, he paused, frowning at first. How was he going to keep his belongings secure when he wasn't home? Certainly out of all the ex-cons being housed there, somebody was a thief. Those types of old habits and lifestyles were hard to break. The last thing he wanted to do was catch a case and land himself back in jail, but he wasn't going to let anyone steal from him either.

"No lock on the door." Amp sighed, shaking his head, but then a slight smile emerged when he realized that for the first time in a long time, he wasn't locked up in a room. His frustration turned to gratitude. The worst times of his life were behind him.

Amp picked up his duffle bag from the chair and carried it over to the closet. He opened the door and heard the melody of the creaking, rusty hinges. Clearly none of the home's original doors had been upgraded. Inside the closet were about ten wire hangers and some linens on the top shelf. Amp hung up the few items he'd stuffed in the bag, then opened the dresser drawer to put away his undergarments. The scent of the old wood reminded him of the dresser he'd had in his room as a kid. His mother kept newspaper in the bottom of each drawer, perhaps as some sort of poor-man's drawer liner.

From the top shelf of the closet he grabbed a towel and wash cloth from the two non-matching sets that were left there for him, and then he headed to the bathroom.Placing the towel and washcloth down on the toilet lid, Amp pulled back the clear plastic shower curtain and turned the single knob, hoping that the temperature indicators weren't reversed. The water shot out of the spigot, pounding onto the blue shower mat. While he waited for the water to hopefully heat up, Amp began to undress.

He pulled his cap off his head, laid it down on the sink, and ran his hands through his unruly hair. He usually liked to keep it edged up, but these past couple of weeks, he'd had more important things on his mind—like being amped up about his release date. Amp ran his hands down his beard. He'd gone into prison clean-faced, like the college boy he was, but he'd had to grow up fast in the joint. His grown-man beard reflected such.

He unbuttoned his sky blue denim-type shirt and slid each muscular arm out, leaving only a white wife-beater underneath. There weren't a lot of mirrors in the joint, so now that he had the opportunity, he took a good look at his reflection. The wife-beater clung to his well-shaped chest and shoulders. His arms were strong and well defined.

Amp was proud of how sculptured his body was. He'd entered the joint at almost twenty-four years old with pretty much the same thin physique he'd had in high school, but he was all man now. Pushing up on thirty years of age, he would definitely not be mistaken for some kid in high school anymore.

He lifted the wife-beater over his head, revealing a chiseled six pack, thick fan-shaped muscles in his chest area, and a large cross tattoo on his chest. He'd had the cross done in prison to remind him that through it all, he was a child of God, and if nobody else was there for him, God always was.

As he kicked off his shoes and socks, he noticed a sheet of steam wavering above the shower curtain, indicating the water was hot. He unbuckled his belt, let his pants drop to the floor, then slid down and stepped out of his box-er-briefs. Standing there naked, Amp Anthony was all man indeed.

He reached down, grabbed his washcloth, then reached into the shower to test the tem-perature. Pulling back the curtain, he stepped into the warm spray.

He stood there for a moment, enjoying the feeling of the water raining down on his torso. For the first time in years, he could feel the real warmth of a hot shower and savor it. In prison, he always had to be aware of his surroundings in order to protect himself and survive. Too many cats had been caught off guard and lived to re-gret it, so Amp had learned to get in and get out fast. Here, he could actually cherish the moment. He closed his eyes and imagined the drops were instead the fingertips of a beautifully skilled masseuse and he was being meticulously mas-saged, muscle after muscle. Slowly, he placed his entire body under the water and allowed it to pour onto his head like rain, washing away yesterday. Today was a new day.

Opening his eyes, Amp grabbed the generic-looking bar of soap and rubbed it into his wash cloth. Just like in prison, there was no shampoo, so he used the bar to clean his face, his body, and his hair. He didn't mind, though, because the scent was refreshing. Just like everything else he'd experienced this day, it was a hell of a lot better than what he'd grown accustomed to over the past four and a half years.

After his shower, Amp dried off then wrapped the towel around his waist. He put on deodorant, brushed his teeth with the brand new toothbrush and toothpaste that had been supplied, then grabbed a bottle of lotion that sat on the back of the toilet tank.

Walking back into his room, Amp's feet sank into the beige carpet. It didn't go unnoticed or unappreciated by Amp that he was now able to shower and walk around barefoot. Good thing, too, because what wasn't in his duffle bag were those prison-issued flip-flops that he'd purposely left behind. How the outside world managed to turn socks and flip-flops into a fashion statement was beyond him. That was a statement Amp never wanted to make again.

As he sat down on the bed and rubbed his body down with lotion, he noticed the open duffle bag he'd left on the floor. The large brown envelope sticking out of the bag was luring him over. Setting the bottle down on the bed, he picked up the envelope and sat back down with it.

Amp held the envelope in his hands for a few more seconds. Was he ready to take his mind back, when his goal was to move forward? He stared at it for a while, until he could no longer resist the urge, and he emptied the contents of the envelope onto his bed. There were several pictures and letters, some unopened and marked "return to sender." Looking at them, he remembered all of his attempts to reach out to his family and to Shannon Ellis, who was injured badly in his crime. He also remembered the sting of each letter being rejected and sent back.

Most of the pictures were of him and his parents, before he went to prison. The photos always left him torn between the joy of the moment in the picture and the reality that he hadn't spoken to them for years, and it wasn't due to a lack of effort on his part. They had made it clear from the returned mail that they wanted nothing to do with him while he was in prison. Amp wondered if he would ever be able to repair the broken pieces within his family and life. Only time would tell.

The one picture that wasn't of his family was of him and Jesse, a childhood friend. When his father put him out, Jesse hadn't hesitated to let Amp crash at his place for a couple months until he could save up enough money to get his own spot. He was a good friend, almost like a brother, the coolest white guy Amp had ever met, but after a while Amp had to keep him at a distance too. Jesse sold dope back in the day, and Amp didn't want anything to do with that.

Amp wondered how Jesse was doing. He prayed for him and for his family often. Hopefully God hadn't been writing "return to sender" on his prayers too.

Inside the envelope there were also a few newspaper clippings. He flipped past these quickly; they were the toughest for Amp to look at because they reflected the darkest times in his life. He had made a choice that he would have to spend the rest of his life trying to make amends for, even after prison. He wasn't ready to face his demons just yet, so he kept it moving.

Amp picked up a couple more pleasant pictures and looked at them, trying to focus on better times. He had read a couple of self-help books in prison that taught him how to have power over his mind by visualizing and focusing on the positive. He often practiced this philosophy in jail to keep his sanity, and was utilizing it now for the same reason. Pulling out a few of the opened letters, he read them over again, just as he had done on more occasions than he could remember. It was no surprise that he practically had them memorized. Reading the "good" letters was almost like hearing his family and friends' voices. Maybe that was why Amp insisted on doing it so often. He sometimes needed to hear voices other than the ones that often taunted him in his head.

When Amp finished reading one letter, he placed it to the side, revealing another newspaper clipping. He froze, staring at the headline as the paper trembled in his hand. Why couldn't he just put it down? Why did he insist on going back in time when he knew all of the hurt and pain it caused? He tried to keep it together by being emotionless, hard, and strong. That is what had protected him while he was in prison.

Yet he was no longer in prison and no one was watching. His eyes filled with tears of shame as he thought back to that night that changed everything. He hadn't mean to hurt her, but he did. He let his family down, his friends, and most of all himself. Amp didn't want to keep revisiting that night. He wanted to stay positive, hopeful for the future, but his conscience wouldn't let him forget all of the damage he had caused in an instant. So much regret.

Amp heard Paul shouting from downstairs. "Lights out in ten minutes." He hadn't realized so much time had passed. He'd sat there reliving his past, almost down to the second it seemed.

Laying on the bed, he closed his eyes, hoping to turn off the barrage of guilt he often unleashed upon himself. He wanted to think about something else, anything else. He was emotionally and spiritually drained.

There was a knock on his door, and then he heard Paul repeating, "Lights out in ten minutes."

"Cool," Amp replied.

He sat up and put all the items back in the envelope, except for a picture and a newspaper clipping. The envelope went into the top dresser drawer, underneath his underwear to conceal it. He stood the photo against the clock.

Pulling out a pair of boxers and a wife-beater, he dropped his towel to the floor. It was nice not to have to look over his shoulder while he got dressed. He hung the towel over the bathroom door to dry, then hit the lights and got into bed.

Picking up the one newspaper article he had not placed back in the envelope, he stared at it, using the light from the moon that was sneaking in between the blinds. Amp knew that one day he would have to right this wrong. He just didn't know how.

It wasn't long before Amp had drifted off into a deep sleep, finally in a bed other than one fit for a seven-year-old, with an inch-thick mattress on top of some wire coils. Unfortunatley, his sleep wasn't as restful as he had hoped for.

Every few minutes Amp shifted from side to side, tossing in the bed, moaning and groaning. The word "No" escaped from his lips. His eyes were closed and there was nothing but darkness, yet they seemed to be wide open to the past. Amp could see everything in his mind's eye happening now—all over again. It was a nightmare. It was a nightmare then, and it was a nightmare now.

Amp's body tensed up as if he were bracing himself for impact. He took in a deep breath. He could hear the screeching sound of tires and then the sound of a loud crash.

Amp shot straight up out of the bed, eyes now wide open. His chest was rising up and down rapidly as he breathed heavily. The things he had just seen in his dream were so vivid, so real.

Momentarily, he wasn't sure where he was. He was haunted by the darkness.

The room was black and silent, with the exception of the sound of Amp's breathing. There was a blur and a stinging in Amp's eyes. Slightly dazed and confused, he ran his hand across his forehead and caught the persperation before it could drip down his eyelids and into his eyes again.

He looked down at his shirt, which was stuck to his skin with moisture. He began to calm down, realizing that he was in his room at the halfway house. It was just another bad dream.

Amp's eyes made their way over to the clock that revealed that it was three a.m. Next they landed on the picture he'd leaned up against the clock. Amp walked over, picked up the picture, and then laid it face down. He had beaten himself up enough for the night. Reading the article had worn him out mentally. Remorse and guilt filled every crevice of his being.

He walked over to the bedroom door and slowly opened it, sticking his head out into the hallway to make sure the coast was clear. All of the other three upstairs bedroom doors were closed. The fifth bedroom in the house, which was Paul's, was downstairs.

Amp padded barefooted down the hallway, the hardwood floor creaking with nearly every step he took. He didn't want to wake any of the other housemates. Of all the rules Paul had beaten him over the head with, he hadn't mentioned whether getting up after lights out was a house violation. Amp hoped not. It wasn't like he was attempting to leave the house.

Making his way into the ample-sized kitchen, Amp grabbed a glass out of the cabinet and filled it with water. He took a sip, then paused, thinking he'd heard something. He listened for a few seconds, but there was nothing but silence. Amp shook off the notion that he'd heard something and finished the much-needed water. He was always dehydrated after his night sweats. Refreshed, he put the glass in the sink and then turned to head back upstairs.

He paused again, certain he'd heard something this time. The sound was coming from the direction of the living room. Walking as quietly as he could, Amp tip-toed into the living room, where he saw Paul.

Paul was in his own little world. Wearing a T-shirt and some pajama pants, he sat in a worn but comfortable-looking La-Z-Boy recliner right next to the stereo system. He was wearing headphones, but Amp could still hear what sounded like some old soul music playing. Paul sat there, none the wiser that he had company, bobbing his head up and down.

When Amp moved a little, Paul must have seen him in his peripheral vision. He turned around, looking startled. He pulled the headphones off his ears.

"You can't sleep either?" Amp asked.

"I told you," Paul said. "We all got shit." He placed the headphones back on his ears and went back to his own little world.

Amp looked at Paul and nodded in agreement. "Good night," he said, even though he knew Paul couldn't hear him. He then headed back upstairs, disappearing back into his own world of memories as well.

Chapter 3

Amp had been notified during breakfast that he needed to wash the dishes after everyone had eaten, so there he stood, elbow deep in suds. He didn't mind though. He had occasionally done kitchen detail in prison, and washing dishes for five or six people was nothing compared to cleaning up after hundreds.

"Just in case you had no idea what to do today, tomorrow, and the day after that," Paul said, entering the kitchen with a piece of paper in hand and then sticking it onto the refrigerator. "Now you do." He turned and looked at Amp. "That is a list of the rest of your chores for the week. You're the new guy, so you're up to bat," Paul informed him. "House tradition."

Shaking his head, Amp wondered if that tradition had just started with him. As he returned to the pile of dishes that needed to be washed, a couple of the other housemates walked over and added more dirty dishes to the stack. Having seen a light at the end of the tunnel just seconds ago, Amp cut his eyes at the growing heap now casting a shadow on that light.

"When I'm done in here—" Amp looked at the pile of dishes again. "If I ever get done in here, I'm gonna get out and put in some job applications."

"That sounds like a plan," Paul said, looking somewhat surprised that Amp was already on the hunt for a job.

"It usually takes the average convict a few days to get up the courage to go tackle the workforce," Paul said frankly.

"Maybe I'm not the average convict," Amp replied.

"We'll see."

"Any suggestions on where to start?" Amp asked.

Paul thought for a quick second. "There's a mall not too far from here, up by the expressway. Lots of stores and shops. There are some restaurants and sports bars over there too."

Amp nodded. "I need to find somewhere to cash my check from my prison job."

"There's a check cashing place over there, if I'm not mistaken."

"Yeah, there is. Right next to the liquor store," one of the housemates chimed in as he scraped his plate into the garbage can and set it on the pile of dishes that seemed like it would never get smaller. "That's the first stop guys from the house usually make after cashing a check anyway." He was laughing, but stopped abruptly once he saw the serious look on Paul's face.

"That's funny to you, Brad?" Paul said sternly.

Amp checked this Brad dude out with a quick once over. Brad was a stoner-looking white dude. If there'd been a comedy club over at that mall, Brad would have fit right in—or at least Brad probably thought he would have. He must have used humor to get by in jail, Amp thought. A person had to use whatever tactic he could to survive in that place.

"You must be the new guy," Brad said to Amp. "I'm Brad." He extended his hand.

With both hands in the dish water, Amp just looked at Brad's hand and left him hanging. He did hit him with the "what up?" head nod though. "Amp," he introduced himself.

"Well, good luck finding a job, Amp," Brad said, not sounding genuine at all. "Everybody here is trying to find a job."

"Some a little harder than others," Paul jumped in. "Speaking of which, when is the last time you put in a job application?"

Brad's eyes immediately shot downward. "Well, uh . . ." Brad hesitated. "I gotta go. I'll catch ya this afternoon, Mr. Harold." He scurried off, bumping into one of the chairs at the table. "Nice to meet you, Amp," he threw over his shoulder before he disappeared from the kitchen.

Paul looked at Amp. He had no words in regards to Brad; he simply shrugged and exited the kitchen as well.

With no more housemates adding to the pile, Amp was finally able to finish the dishes—or so he thought. Just as he turned around to go get ready for his job search, one more of his housemates entered the kitchen with a plate and a glass. "Damn."

About ten minutes later, Amp entered the living room, heading for the door. Paul was sitting on the couch, reading the newspaper.

Looking over the top of his paper, Paul said, "I didn't mention it earlier, but if you get any crazy ideas about not coming back . . ."

Amp, who was almost out the door, turned around to face Paul. "Mr. Harold, I've been in prison for the last fifty-four months. I ain't doing nothing to mess this up."

"That's good to hear," Paul said, even though he'd heard it before and only half believed the new housemate. Paul didn't put anything past any of those cats. It was his job not to.

"Besides," Amp added, "I ain't one to miss a meal either. I'll be back by lunch time."

"All right, now that I believe." He chuckled. "You got your ID, social security card, and all your paperwork?"

"Yep," Amp said as he walked out the door.

There was a computer in the house that the parolees were allowed to use with a twenty-minute time limit, so Amp had looked up the directions to the mall before he left the house. Now, he passed by the bus stop where he could have gotten a ride to the mall, preferring to walk. He wanted to save what little money he had, and it wasn't that far anyway. Plus, it had been quite a long time since he had been able to walk anywhere alone. This walk was free, literally, in every sense of the word.

The look on Amp's face said it all as he walked on the sidewalk along the busy street. He was enjoying the bright rays of sunshine, even if he had to shield his eyes every now and then to see where he was going. He was also enjoying the warmth of the rays on his skin and relishing the sound of the cars whizzing by. Almost always in serious mode and ready to handle business, for once Amp was relaxed, letting his mind, body, and soul absorb all the sights and the sounds, so much so that it had subconsciously put a smile on his face. His outside was now reflecting how he felt on the inside.

The last few years of his life might not have been good, but if the sun shining, the birds singing, and the sweet smell of fresh air were any indication of what lay ahead, today was going to be a good day.

"Can I help you?" The young Caucasian woman behind the counter at the dollar store had a cheery smile on her face as she waited to serve Amp. She looked as though that was what she was born to do: wait on customers in a dollar store with a permanent smile on her face.

"I was wondering if you guys were hiring," Amp said.

"Well, uh . . ." All of a sudden that smile dropped right off her face. Just a few seconds ago when she thought she'd only have to entertain Amp for the next five minutes, she was as happy as a Jay bird. Now that there was a chance that she might have to spend eight hours working next to him every day, she didn't look so happy anymore.

"If so, I'd like an application," Amp said, ignoring her change in demeanor. "I'll work part-time, weekends, anything."

What was left of her smile looked forced as she said nothing.

"Do you have any applications?" Amp said , wondering if there was something wrong with this woman.

"Well, no . . ." she started, trailing off. The woman's mouth hung open as she contemplated her next words. Amp noticed her eyes darting over toward the corner of the store, then darting back at him. He turned in the direction where she'd been looking, and noticed a small desk with a computer. Taped to the desk was a small sign that read: ONLINE APPLICATIONS. If the woman hadn't been so obvious, Amp would have never even noticed. She could have simply told him they weren't hiring and he would have been on his merry way.

"We don't have any applications . . . at least not any paper ones. Everything is done electronically now. On the internet." Apparently she didn't want to straight out lie, especially now since Amp had seen the computer.

"So I just go over there to fill out an online application?" Amp asked as he started toward the computer.

"No! Well, yes, but uh . . . that computer is down." Her smile was back, but it looked a little devious now, like she was proud that she'd thought quickly on her feet.

Amp was onto her now and realized what type of game she was trying to play with him. Instead of getting angry, he just decided to play along. "Oh, really? The computer is down, huh? Well, you know I'm pretty good with computers," he lied just to mess with her. "It's a trade I learned in prison."

"Prison?" She swallowed hard and her eyes bucked. The poor white girl's skin turned as red as cherry Kool-Aid.

"Oh, yeah, I served a little time." He enjoyed toying with her, but hid it well.

"Uh, well . . ." Her nerves had her shaking. The blond hairs on her arms stood up. "I can't allow you to touch that computer. Like I said, it's out of order and besides, I don't think they're hiring anyway. They just hired two people last week." She snapped her finger. "Darn, sorry about your timing."

"Is that so?"

She nodded. Amp noticed the beads of sweat trickling down her forehead. If she had spoken another word, she probably would have thrown up right there on the counter.

"Then I guess I'll try back again, what, say next week?" Amp stared hard, knowing how uncomfortable it made her. "I mean, you never know. You guys could be hiring again sooner than you think."

She looked too nervous to speak at this point. Amp considered messing with the lady further, but decided against it. He really had better things to do.

"You know what? Forget it." He gave a Kanye shrug and left the store. Clearly he wasn't going to get hired at that place, so he headed for his next opportunity for employment.

Amp hit up several more spots, and lunch had come and gone by the time he made it back to the halfway house. Amp entered the front door. The subconscious smile that had been on his face earlier that morning was now replaced with a very conscious frown.

"Don't worry, Annie, the sun will come out tomorrow," Brad joked. He was on the couch, watching television along with another house-mate named Melvin.

Melvin was an average-looking cat weighing about a buck fifty. Tall and slender, he stood about six feet six inches tall, which meant 150 pounds didn't look like much on him. It was safe to say that once upon a time he'd probably battled an addiction.

Melvin snorted at Brad's comment.

"Looks like somebody had a rough day," Brad said, elbowing Melvin while nodding at Amp.

"I ain't in the mood, man," Amp said to Brad in a cold tone.

Paul entered from the kitchen and caught Amp's comment. "How'd it go?" he asked, even though it was pretty obvious from Amp's demeanor. "You weren't back at lunch time, so I figured . . ." His words trailed off as he waited to let Amp reply to his initial inquiry.

Amp answered with a look of disdain, as Brad continued to laugh about the situation. Amp shot Brad a "leave me the hell alone before I whoop your ass" look, and that shut him up.

"I think I'm gonna go stretch my legs," Brad said to no one in particular as he headed for the kitchen.

"So, did you hit that mall?" Paul resurrected the conversation.

"I went to more than thirty stores and restaurants over there. Most of 'em wouldn't even give me an application."

Amp wasn't exaggerating either. Some places clearly had HELP WANTED signs in their windows, but when Amp asked for a job application, he was told, "Sorry, sir. We're not hiring right now." Then, of course, there was the whole issue at the dollar store.

Paul looked sympathetically at Amp for a second and then said, "Come here. I want to show you something."

Amp sighed, not in any kind of mood for show and tell. He just wanted to go to his room and be left alone right now. Paul's statement wasn't exactly a request, though, so Amp followed Paul, who led him up the steps.

They entered Amp's room. A puzzled look pieced itself together on Amp's face as he wondered what in the world Paul could possibly have to show him in his own room.

"Come on in here." Paul directed Amp into the bathroom.

Amp was a little suspicious. He was fresh out of the joint; he couldn't be too trusting too quickly.

"Stand in front of the mirror," Paul ordered him.

Amp did as he was told.

"Look." Paul pointed at Amp's reflection.

Amp looked, but wondered what there was to see besides the same face he looked at every morning. Truth be told, Amp didn't really care for mirrors. Guilt and regret met him there daily, so unless it was necessary, he avoided them.

"Would *you* hire you?" Paul asked. "Huh?"

Amp didn't respond, still not sure what point Paul was trying to make.

"Your shirt is too big," Paul pointed out. "And your jeans are baggy."

Amp's jeans were quite baggy. They hung so low that his back pockets could still be seen hanging below the hem of his oversized shirt. Amp pulled his pants up and tightened his belt. He definitely didn't want anyone to confuse his baggy pants for a sag. Back in the joint, if a cat sagged his pants, it meant that he was advertising his interest in male sexual interaction. Amp definitely wasn't about that life, so he made certain that he didn't dress like he was.

"Then there's that beard of yours." Paul had a disapproving look on his face. "I don't understand what this whole thing with these full beards is with these young cats. Trim that thing. Clean it up or something." He pointed to Amp's head. "And you got that cap on your head. So I ask you again: Would you hire you to run a cash register or to work at a department store?"

Amp took a really hard look at his overall appearance and concluded that Paul was right. He did not look like he was there to get a job. "I guess not."

Paul opened the medicine cabinet, pulled out a pair of clippers, and extended them to Amp. "You know how to use these?" Paul asked.

Amp took the clippers from him. "Yeah. I was a barber on the inside. That's the only thing that kept them fools off my back."

Amp thought back to his first year in prison. An old inmate by the name of Martel had told him that he better get a hustle or a trade fast. Making yourself valuable was the only surefire way of not having your manhood taken. Amp had years of experience cutting hair, and he knew right away what his trade should be. He had been saving his money from his prison job, so when another inmate was being released, Amp bought his clippers. He had to clean them, fix them up, and sharpen the blade, but they did the job.

Amp's timing couldn't have been better. One afternoon, Bull, the number one guy in the biggest black gang in the prison, stopped by Amp's cell with two equally menacing members of his clique.

Bull stepped inside the cell, and Amp could tell right away that he was not to be fucked with.

"Word is you're the new barber," Bull said, looking Amp dead in the eyes. Amp knew he had to look him right back in his eyes. It was a respect thing, and whatever happened next, it was going to be said that Amp was not a punk.

"I am," Amp replied. "I'm cold with the clippers. You need a cut?"

"Yeah, I do, but I don't pay for haircuts in *my* prison."

Amp's heart was now damn near beating out of his chest. He knew this situation could go bad fast, so he glanced around the cell for a weapon. Finding nothing, he faced Bull, struggling to hide his nervousness.

Then Bull surprised him with a deal: "I'm going to offer you the same deal I gave the last barber. Twenty percent of the money you make cutting heads gets kicked back to me. Also, me and both of my generals here get a free cut once a week." His tone was all business.

"What do I get out of the deal?" Amp asked, maintaining his confident air but still being respectful.

Bull replied without blinking an eye. "We guarantee no one tries to rape you in the shower and nobody fucks with you on the yard. Deal?"

Amp didn't need long to think it over. "Deal," Amp said, never breaking his eye contact with Bull.

Bull nodded in agreement, then just as quickly as they had entered, they were gone.

For the rest of his stay, Amp kept his end of the deal. He paid Bull his twenty percent every week and made sure Bull and his two generals always had a fresh cut. In return, nobody messed with Amp. The one guy who was dumb enough to try it ended up beaten half to death in the shower. After that, no one else looked twice at Amp.

Amp looked at the clippers with admiration. They had saved his ass, literally.

"Yeah, I'm handy with these," he said with a little smirk.

"Good, use them," Paul said, nodding at the clippers. "One more thing: Part of the reason that most of those stores wouldn't give you an application could possibly be your energy. When most guys are first released from prison, they are standoffish and defensive, like they're waiting for something bad to happen—or like they are the bad thing that's going to happen. You're not in prison anymore, so if you are serious about finding a job, you need to keep that in mind."

Amp nodded in agreement. He had to admit that pre-jail, he was a far more outgoing and likeable dude. Sadly, his life had been drastically changed, mainly due to the fact that he had drastically changed someone else's.

Paul gave Amp a nod of support and turned to leave.

Amp stopped him. "Hey, can I, uh . . . I need to borrow a shirt with a collar. Please."

Paul crossed his arms. "I thought you were cashing your check."

"I did. That's all the money I got. Didn't wanna spend it on no shirt."

Paul let out a breath. "I got one you can borrow. I'll bring it to your room."

"Thanks."

"No problem. And hopefully you'll have better luck tomorrow," Paul said then left.

Amp plugged in the clippers. Looking at himself in the mirror again, Amp thought, *I don't need luck. I need a job.*

The sound of the clippers buzzed for the next few minutes as Amp cleaned up his appearance, hoping his transformation wouldn't be in vain.

Chapter 4

"You look like you work at Best Buy," Brad said to Amp when he entered the kitchen.

"I wish," Amp replied as he looked down at the polo shirt, tucked into jeans that were now pulled up to his waist. Amp ran his hand down his clean-shaven face to his nicely trimmed beard. No skull cap today, as his hair was shaped up and brushed.

Paul walked in the room carrying the day's newspaper. He spotted Amp and did a double take. "I see the shirt fits."

Amp tugged at the navy blue polo. It wasn't an oversized tee, that's for sure, and he wasn't one hundred percent comfortable in it, but hopefully it would serve its purpose. This wasn't about being comfortable. This was about getting employed.

"You must have been tired," Paul said. "You slept right through breakfast. Brad took your chores this morning, so you have his tomorrow."

Amp looked at the cleared stove and the clean breakfast dishes drying in the rack. "It's cool. I'll just grab some fruit and a bottle of water real quick."

Paul nodded and then went back into the living room.

Amp walked over and opened the fridge, grabbing a couple of small plums and a bottle of water before he headed for the front door to go get started on putting in some job applications. He was feeling good and had renewed energy this morning.

"You going to get 'em today, huh?" Paul asked Amp as he walked through the living room, taking a bite of a plum. Paul could see the fight and determination on Amp's face.

"Yep. I'm going back to every store that wouldn't give me an application yesterday, and I'm putting in an application this time." Amp figured with his change in appearance, they wouldn't even recognize him from the day before. "I'll be back later." Amp walked out to the porch, then stopped and looked back through the screen door, the corners of his mouth raised into a grin. "I'm coming back here with a job." Amp just felt it in his bones that today was the day, and even though he hadn't verbalized it, he appreciated Paul's help in making it possible.

"I'm sure you will." Paul nodded in agreement.

Hours later, Amp was making his way back up the cement steps to the porch of the halfway house. He stopped on the faded gray concrete porch with his teeth clenched, wanting to break something. Amp felt like a failure, even more deflated and frustrated than he had yesterday. Today he had done everything right, but as soon as each employer found out he was an ex-con, he encountered the same rejection, which made him feel hopeless. He began to think about some of the guys in the prison who were released only to return again because they resorted to stealing when they struggled to make a living the legitimate way. Amp knew that would not be his fate, but at this moment thoughts of doubt and fear began creeping in.

The sound of someone snickering disturbed his thoughts. He looked up and saw Brad.

They locked eyes through the screen door, but when Brad saw that he was caught clownin' Amp, he swiftly got off the couch and left the room. Amp just gritted his teeth and shook his head. That Brad guy needed to chill out before shit got real.

Amp went inside, where he saw Paul sitting on the faux suede couch and another housemate in one of the chairs, watching TV. There was an open file on the oval-shaped coffee table in front of Paul, like he'd been doing some paperwork. Paul rested back on the couch, giving Amp his full attention.

Amp could tell that Paul was waiting to get the details of his day's efforts, but he was not in the mood to talk. He just kept walking, final destination his bedroom, so he could shower and call it a day—a not so good day at that.

"Any better luck today?" Paul asked, not letting Amp get away without providing an update.

Amp stopped halfway through the living room. "No. I filled out thirteen applications and had a few on-the-spot interviews. I was honest. Told them I was a felon on my applications. They couldn't get me out of the store fast enough after that."

"It may take a minute, but you'll find something," Paul said, and then went back to his paperwork. His affirmative words were far more confident than Amp felt.

"Nah, Brad was right," Amp said. "Ain't nobody going to hire me." Feeling mentally exhausted and dejected, he continued his trek to his room.

"I put a plate in the refrigerator for you," Paul said without looking up from his file.

Amp wasn't hungry, not for food anyway. He was hungry to start a fresh life, to get a job so that he could get out of the halfway house and make amends for what he had done. He had wasted too many years in the pen, and his need to be a productive part of society again was within reach, if only he could catch a break. For now, though, he just had to worry about tomorrow, hoping its results wouldn't mirror those of the past two days. That glimmer of hope in Amp's eyes was getting smaller by the day.

The next morning Amp came down the steps wearing a wife-beater, basketball shorts, and some running shoes. The house was pretty quiet and empty. Everyone must have been on their daily grind. The front door was wide open. Amp walked out onto the porch and saw Paul sitting there in one of the white plastic chairs on his right, reading the morning news.

"Is there a park somewhere close by?" Amp asked.

"Atfield Park is about a mile up the road," Paul replied. "Opposite direction of the shopping center."

"Cool. I'll be back." Amp stepped down off the porch, did some quick stretching, then took off up the street.

He wasn't a quitter, and he wasn't going to give up after just two days of job hunting, so he wasn't completely washing his hands of finding a job. He just needed to take a breather to get his mind right. He figured he'd get his workout on.

Amp started out with a light jog. The wind seemed to be pushing him along. Not bound by thirty-foot tall fences, he decided to turn it up. The faster he ran, the more free he felt. In his mind he was sixteen again, with no cares, no worries, so he let his legs carry him as fast as they could. His breathing was rhythmic, and he was in a groove now, to the point to where he almost ran past the park.

The run had definitely helped, giving him great clarity and tranquility, just as it always did. It was his therapy. Before going to jail, Amp had been a star athlete at school, excelling at basketball, cross country, and track. This morning run reminded him of days when he was a winner, when championship trophies were regularly displayed on his living room mantle. He was ready to live in the light of greatness again, but right now, with no one trying to give him an opportunity, he definitely needed to figure out what his next move should be. It was going to take more than a jog for Amp to get his life back on track.

Amp slowed his pace and jogged over to the monkey-bars, where he stretched out a little more and did an array of push-ups, pull-ups, and sit-ups. With every set, Amp visualized all of the "no's" and brush-offs he had been subjected to over the last couple of days. Then his thoughts traveled further back in time, and Shannon's face popped up in his mind. He double-timed his push-ups, trying to erase the image. Her face disappeared, only to be replaced by flashbacks of the disappointed expressions of his mother and father in the courtroom. Amp drew in deep, angry breaths and went even harder with each exercise. It felt good to take his frustration out on something. He needed this.

A few people watched him from a distance, including a woman pushing her infant in a stroller, who could barely keep her eyes on the pathway as she admired Amp's immaculately sculpted frame. Amp was too focused to notice. As far as he was aware, it was just him and the trees.

Amp was covered in sweat as he stood up, dusted off his hands, and caught his breath. He felt better now—calmer, stronger. The determination was back in his eyes. He didn't care how far he had to search; he was going to find a job. His life depended on it.

He also decided that in order to move forward, he would need to let go of the past. He could only do that if he talked to Shannon and tried to make things right. First, he would have to find her.

After an intense workout, he headed back toward the house. On the way he noticed a small, run-down convenience store. Thirsty as hell but unwilling to drink from the filthy fountain in the park, he stopped in to grab something to drink.

"Get out! You steal from me!" an older Asian guy shouted out. He was ushering a young black man out of the store, nearly running Amp over as he entered.

"Come on, Mr. Lam," the black dude pleaded. "You know I wouldn't play you like dat."

"You steal from me!" Mr. Lam continued. "You fired. No come back here again. Fired! You come back, I call police. You go to jail."

Amp watched the young, alleged thief walk away while Mr. Lam stood there pointing, ranting and raving, now in his native tongue. If Amp had been a cartoon character, a little light bulb would have hung over his head as an idea popped into his mind.

Mr. Lam reentered the store, still fussing under his breath.

"Excuse me, sir," Amp said, trying to get the store owner's attention.

Mr. Lam was too busy muttering to himself.

"Uh, excuse me . . ." His eyes happened upon the man's name tag. "Excuse me, Mr. Lam."

Upon hearing his name, Mr. Lam turned and faced the customer he was noticing for the first time. "Yes," he snapped, still very much agitated.

Instinctually, Amp was about to snap back, but then he remembered what Paul had told him about his attitude. He cleared his throat and tried again. "Uh, I'm sorry to bother you."

Mr. Lam's eyes traveled down to Amp's workout clothes, which were now covered in sweat. Another one of Paul's lessons—the one about appearance—came to Amp's mind. He wasn't exactly dressed professionally, but at least it wasn't saggy jeans. He straightened himself up as best he could before sharing his idea with Mr. Lam. "My name is Amp Anthony. Forgive my appearance. I was out jogging."

Mr. Lam nodded and said in broken English, "Come on and get on wit' it. I very upset right now. This not good time."

"If you just fired him"—Amp pointed toward the door—"does that mean that you have a job opening?"

A look came across Mr. Lam's face, as if for the first time he was realizing he was in a fix. He was pissed, but there were a lot of empty shelves and racks that needed inventory placed on them before the neighborhood kids got out of school. He looked Amp up and down again, sizing him up.

"Look," Amp continued, "I'll work hard. I'm reliable, and I don't steal."

Mr. Lam still didn't seem too sure about taking Amp up on his offer.

Amp looked around the store. It was the average corner store with a few aisles, a large cooler, candy and gum rack by the register, and a doorway leading to the office and storage in the back. "I can stock the shelves and the cooler, sweep, mop, take out the trash, and work the register. I can do it. I need a job, sir." Amp's voice didn't relay the desperation he was feeling in his heart, but his eyes did.

Mr. Lam took one more look at Amp, then glanced around his store at all the work that his former employee would no longer be doing. It was definitely more than one old man could handle by himself. He finally said, "Can you start today?"

"Yes! Yes, sir," Amp said, wanting to burst at the seams. Finally, the break that he desperately needed.

Looking down at his soggy workout gear, he asked, "Can I shower first and put on something more appropriate? I live like five minutes from here." Amp was eager to impress his new boss. He wanted him to know that he had made the right choice in trusting him.

"Be back in thirty minutes," Mr. Lam said.

"Thirty minutes," Amp assured him and then quickly dashed out the door.

"Hey!" Mr. Lam stopped him in his tracks. "And no play me like dat." He pointed, squinting his eyes for emphasis.

"No, sir," Amp said, trying to keep from laughing at the Asian man's misuse of slang. "I wouldn't play you like that." He turned and raced happily back to the halfway house.

Chapter 5

Amp bounded up the porch steps to the halfway house, tripping and darn near falling into the screen door. He'd run all the way home from Mr. Lam's store full speed. If he hadn't needed a shower before, he certainly was in need of one now, as sweat poured down his face.

He entered to the usual scene: a couple of housemates glued in front of the television and Paul with newspaper in hand.

"Damn, the only time I see cats huffing and puffing like that is when they're running from the cops," one of the housemates said. "You all right, man?"

"Yeah, you all right?" Paul stood, looking concerned. He leaned forward, peeping through the screen door as if checking to see if, in fact, the police were close behind the out-of-breath parolee.

Amp, trying to catch his breath, nodded.

"Good, because I need to talk to you about something," Paul said.

"Can it wait? I got somewhere I have to be," Amp huffed out, finally starting to get his breathing leveled.

Paul flexed up a little, and Amp realized that his words might have been interpreted as disrespectful. Granted, he wasn't in prison anymore and didn't have to be told his every move, but Paul was still the man in charge and not someone he needed to piss off.

Amp offered, "I got a job. I start in thirty minutes." He looked up at the clock. "Make that twenty-five minutes."

"Twenty-five minutes?" Paul said, surprised. "Then why are you just standing here? Go get yourself together."

As Amp headed up to his room, he heard Paul say, "Wouldn't hurt for a couple of y'all to pay attention to Amp. That's a young man making it happen and not making excuses."

Amp closed his door, smiling with satisfaction over the fact that Paul had given him that recognition aloud. He had achieved what he had set out to do, and he was proud of himself. This would be the first step in getting back on the right track and walking into his destiny.

***

"Oh, you come back," Mr. Lam said to Amp when he returned to the store thirty minutes later, now showered, changed, and eager to start earning a paycheck.

Amp nodded and then rubbed his hands together, eager to get started. This wasn't a major career move, but it was a start. Someone was giving him a chance, and he would seize the opportunity.

Mr. Lam proceeded to show Amp around the store and explain his duties. On occasion Amp had difficulty understanding what Mr. Lam was saying because his accent was so heavy, but for the most part, his tasks were self-explanatory. Within ten minutes Mr. Lam put him to work, carrying boxes from the storage room, stacking shelves, and then fixing up displays. Next was cleanup duty: sweeping, mopping, and dusting. Amp hit every corner of the store, from the bathroom to the storage room to the office. Even if that dude Mr. Lam had thrown out hadn't been fired for stealing, he should have been fired for doing a piss poor job at keeping the store up. Amp could only imagine the last time the tasks he'd done today had been performed up to par.

When he saw that Amp was a good worker, Mr. Lam decided to train him on the cash register, allowing him to do a couple of transactions.

After a long, hard day, a worn-out Amp said, "All right then, Mr. Lam. I'll see you tomorrow."

Mr. Lam nodded without looking up from the cash register drawer where he was counting the day's profits.

As Amp was stepping out the door, Mr. Lam called out to him.

Now what? Amp thought. He'd done workouts that didn't have his body aching as much as it was now. Just five minutes ago Mr. Lam had told him to call it a day. What else, in that short a period of time, could he have possibly thought of that couldn't wait until tomorrow?

"Yes?" Amp turned to Mr. Lam, trying not to sound edgy.

"Good job. Store look nice."

Amp left the store with a smile on his face.

By the time Amp walked through the front door of the house, he was about ready to collapse. He definitely could have skipped exercising today. His time at the store had been a workout in itself.

"How was your first day being employed?" Paul asked Amp as he entered the kitchen and went straight to the fridge to get a bottle of water.

Brad, Melvin, and two other housemates were sitting at the kitchen table engaged in a game of spades.

"It was busy, but good," Amp replied, twisting the cap off of the bottle of water and drinking some. Amp took a seat at the only vacant chair at the kitchen table. "I did twice as much work for thirty cents a day when I was inside. I can definitely handle this." He took another swig of water.

"Really? I can't tell by the way you guzzling down that water. Looks like the store owner worked you half to death."

Melvin chuckled under his breath.

Paul snapped his finger. "Oh, yeah. I wanted to tell you that your parole officer will be here tomorrow morning."

Amp figured that must have been what Paul wanted to talk to him about earlier. "Okay. I work from noon to nine tomorrow, so as long as he doesn't make me late . . ." Amp stood up, drank the last of the water, and threw the empty bottle into the trash can.

"Recycle bin," Paul reminded him.

Amp picked up the bottle and put it in the correct bin. "Any leftovers from dinner?" he asked, his grumbling stomach reminding him that he hadn't eaten since the morning's plums.

Brad looked up from his hand of cards. "Yeah, but Melvin cooked, so you better bless your food."

"Shut up, man. I can cook," Melvin said, twisting up his face.

"We'll see," Amp said as he fixed himself a plate.

He gobbled the baked chicken, rice, and corn on the cob. It didn't taste half bad, though Amp barely noticed because he ate it so fast. He was starving, plus he just wanted to hurry up and finish so he could go lay down. He was so intent on making a good first impression with Mr. Lam that he hadn't even taken a lunch break. After a hard workout and a long day's work, his body needed the rest. Maybe the visions that sometimes disrupted his sleep wouldn't tonight.

The next morning, Amp had breakfast duty, so he prepared some grits, toast, turkey bacon, and scrambled eggs. Well rested, he could actually take time and eat at a normal pace. He enjoyed every bite of his meal, especially the tasty buttered grits, seasoned with salt and pepper, which reminded him of how his mom used to make it. He really missed her. In addition to being an amazing cook who could even make broccoli taste good, she was an amazing caregiver. She had the best hugs that made Amp feel safe and protected.

Amp's mother was another reason he was going to have to keep his nose clean. He thought that if he got out and got his life together, he might be able to reopen those lines of communication and eventually rebuild the relationship.

As Amp was finishing up the last of the breakfast dishes he'd washed, he heard a knock at the door. The apple-shaped kitchen clock that hung over the entry doorway told him it was almost ten o'clock, so he hoped it was his parole officer at the door. That would give him plenty of time to holler at him and then get to work on time, possibly getting in a workout beforehand—although yesterday's aches and pains had him reconsidering the whole exercise idea.

Amp folded the dish towel, laid it on the counter, and then went to answer the door. Through the screen he saw a forty-year-old, uptight-looking white guy. On second thought, maybe it would be better if this dude wasn't his parole officer. There was just something about him that made Amp think dealing with him wasn't going to be pleasurable; but the same way everybody was prejudging him on his job search, he didn't want to be a hypocrite and do it to someone else, so he brushed away any preconceived notions about the man.

"Yeah," Amp said, opening the screen door and stepping out onto the porch.

"I'm here to see Amp Anthony," the guest announced.

"Morning. I'm Amp."

Not extending his hand or even acknowledging Amp's greeting, the gentleman got right down to business. "I'm Arthur Barrett. I'm your parole officer. How are you adjusting?"

"Fine," Amp replied.

"Good. The less I hear about you, the better." Mr. Barrett looked Amp over.

Amp was dressed as if he had someplace to be, which was a little unusual. It was pretty typical for a parole officer to show up to meet with a client at this time of morning and find him still in boxer shorts, wiping sleep out of his eyes.

"What do you have planned for today?" Mr. Barrett asked.

"I'm debating about going to run to the park to get my workout in. Then I'm headed to the market I work at for the rest of the day."

"Job already?" Mr. Barrett opened the case folder he'd had tucked under his armpit.

"Yep." While Mr. Barrett jotted down notes in the file, Amp continued. He wanted to get down to business, too, so that he could go on about his day. "Paul said I was going to be taking a drug test today?" Amp was anxious to get the test over with. He knew he was clean; he just needed everybody else to know as well.

"You will take one," Mr. Barrett said without even looking up from the file he was still scribbling in. "But not today. That's why it's called a random drug test."

Sarcastic ass, Amp thought, but of course that wasn't something he'd ever voice. He wasn't trying to get on this guy's bad side. "Okay. Either way it's cool. I don't mess with nothing anyway."

"Keep it that way." Mr. Barrett closed up the file and tucked it back underneath his armpit. He looked up at his client like it was the first time he was even acknowledging that a human being had been standing in front of him. Everything just seemed so robotic with him. Different day, another black felon. "I'll see you soon."

"Yeah. See you soon," Amp replied as Mr. Barrett turned and walked off the porch.

His encounter with Mr. Barrett had made him a little uptight. He didn't want to go to work on edge, so blowing off some steam by exercising would be a good idea after all.

Amp stepped into the yard and stretched for a few seconds. As he watched Mr. Barrett get inside his car and pull off, he couldn't get the parole officer's last words to him out of his head. *"I'll see you soon."* It was a simple phrase, but somehow, coming from Barrett, it felt like there was a hint of a threat behind it.

Chapter 6

After finishing up his stretches, Amp headed to the park to repeat the same workout as the day before. He'd not only felt good after yesterday's workout, but he'd ended up landing a job. Surely the actual workout itself hadn't brought Amp any type of magic luck, but feeling good afterward helped him maintain a confident attitude that had him speak up at the opportune moment. Who knew what today would bring?

"Excuse me. I don't mean to interrupt your workout."

Amp was in the middle of his push-ups when he looked up to see a set of long, roasted almond brown legs in a set of sexy heels. He knew nothing about the latest fashion when it came to women's shoes, but those five-inch shiny nude pumps with red bottoms that he was looking at had to be something a lot of women would sacrifice a month's salary for.

Amp ceased his workout and stood up, brushing the dirt off his hands as he gave his attention to the well-dressed woman in front of him. She looked to be in her late thirties or early forties and very attractive. "No problem," Amp said. "How can I help you?"

"I was wondering . . ." she started and then paused. "Wait. I'm being rude. My name is Mary Fox. My friends call me Madam." Madam extended her hand with freshly manicured nails, her middle finger donning a diamond ring that had more than likely been custom made. This woman, with her shoulder-length brown hair with golden highlights, not one hair out of place, looked like the type who preferred one-of-a-kinds.

Amp shook her hand. *Soft. Figures.* Madam definitely didn't look like she enjoyed getting her hands dirty; yet she had that edge about her that said if she had to, she would in a heartbeat.

"Nice to meet you, Madam. I'm Amp."

"Well, Amp, I usually eat my lunch here." She looked around, quickly taking in the still atmosphere. "It's peaceful."

Amp looked around and nodded in agreement. He was almost surprised to meet someone who seemed to appreciate the natural surroundings just as much as he did as a newly released prisoner. Then again, women were more apt to be one with nature anyway, thanks to Oprah.

"I've seen you working out here a couple times now." Madam was not discreet in giving Amp the once over. He noticed. It was less like she was checking him out, though, and more like she was inspecting him. Like he was a piece of meat in the butcher shop and she was the inspector hired to make sure all meat being sold was grade A. "What do you do, if you don't mind me asking?"

"Nothing major. I work at a convenience store," Amp admitted without hesitation. He wasn't one of those brothers who tried to be something that he wasn't in order to impress a female. Some dudes might have gone as far as to tell her that they were the manager, or even owned the store, but Amp wasn't that type of guy. He didn't need to be. As a six foot three inch black male with a killer smile and a gladiator physique, he knew the mass appeal that he had amongst women. Besides, Madam looked as though neither of those exaggerations would have impressed her any more or any less. She also wasn't giving off that kind of vibe toward Amp anyway. She appeared to be genuinely interested in just the question she'd asked him.

"Why do you ask?" Amp inquired.

"I own a couple of clubs, and I could use a man like you." Once again, Madam scanned Amp's body with her eyes, as if she had to be sure he had passed her initial inspection.

"Thanks, but I already have a job, and I don't wanna mess that up." A bird in the hand was definitely worth two in the bush as far as Amp was concerned. Mr. Lam had been willing to give him a chance on the spot with no resume, interview, or anything like that. He wasn't about to bail on him after only one day in order to go work for someone else, especially having a felony record to worry about.

"I hear you." Madam nodded. "Well, here." She reached into her black leather tote and then handed him a business card. "If you change your mind, and I really hope you do, call me."

Amp put the card in his pocket and watched Madam sashay up the walking path toward the street. She took her key fob in hand and aimed it at a cream-colored Aston Martin customized convertible with hot red interior seating. Amp heard the car chirp as Madam stepped off the curb and opened the driver's side door.

She looked straight at Amp, as if she knew he'd be looking, and waved as she got in her car. Amp had been watching her indeed. Madam was a nice interruption from his workout. He wasn't watching her because he was digging her, though. For Amp, beautiful women had been a dime a dozen before he entered the pen. Now he had decided that he would make better choices for his entire life, including choosing a woman, so he wasn't going to be blown away by the first pretty face he saw. He was, however, taken in by the level of class she displayed, and the fact that she had her own was even more impressive. Business owner, nice ride, tight shoe game: this Madam looked like a force to be reckoned with.

Amp didn't wait for her to drive off before he went back to his workout. If she ate her lunch at the park on the regular like she had claimed, he was sure he'd see her again, and vice versa.

Later on that afternoon, Amp was behind the counter at the store, with his back to the door, taking inventory of the cigarettes that were shelved behind the counter.

Amp heard someone enter the store and say, "Yo, my man. I need a pack of blunts."

He grabbed a pack then turned around and threw the blunts on the counter to ring them up. "That will be three-oh-seven," Amp said, looking up at the customer for the first time.

"Jesse? Jesse McLain?" It had been a few years since he'd seen him, but Amp would know that face anywhere. It was one of his best childhood friends.

The customer did a double take. "Amp! Aww, hell naw." It was Jesse indeed.

The two old friends gave each other some dap. Jesse was dressed a little more dapper than Amp remembered his style to be, with his expensive designer jeans and a fitted V-neck thermal shirt that showed off his muscular frame. Back in the day Jesse wore whatever his older brother had grown out of, even if it was still two sizes too big. Jesse certainly wasn't in anybody's hand-me-downs today. His outfit was complemented by a two-carat diamond earring in his left ear, a nice gold chain with a moderately-sized but clearly expensive medallion, and a matching watch on his wrist.

"Man, when you get out?" Jesse asked.

"A couple weeks ago."

"Oh, word? How's the fam doing?"

Amp took a pause, caught off guard by Jesse's inquiry as well as the familiar sense of loss that rose in him whenever he thought of his family.

He shook it off the best he could. "Your guess is as good as mine. I ain't heard from them since I went in." He changed the subject quickly. "So, what you been up to?"

"You ain't heard?" Jesse puffed out his chest with pride. "I'm killin' 'em out here." He looked around to make sure no one was listening. Mr. Lam was in the back office and there were no other customers in the store. It was just the two of them, so he continued. "Any party favor you can name, I sell it, a lot of it. And it's paying off pretty well." He nodded over his shoulder toward the outside.

Amp looked out the window and saw Jesse's black Next Generation Range Rover with 22-inch Redbourne Viceroy silver wheels rims. Jesse had not only stepped up his wardrobe game, but his ride was an improvement from the pair of sneakers that was his former means of transportation. Amp knew he'd sold a little back in the day, but obviously he'd come way up in the game.

"Daaaaamn," Amp said, admiring the vehicle.

"You like that, huh?" Jesse rubbed his chin with his index finger and thumb. "I can put you on, bruh. Just say the word. You know you're like family to me. We grew up on these blocks together. I got you. You don't have to do this low-end shit." He raised his arms, looking around the store. " 'Cause working here definitely ain't gon' put you in one of those." He nodded toward his vehicle again, and Amp's eyes followed.

That was one hell of a ride. Amp could see himself pushing something like that—but at what cost? Amp knew that he had promised himself and God that he would never be confined to those prison walls again, and he meant it. No possession in the world was worth his freedom. That was too great a price! He took in a deep breath and then exhaled.

"I can't, man. I got three months at this halfway house I'm staying at and then I'm free. I can't take that chance, bruh. Good lookin' out though."

"I feel you," Jesse said. "Well, take my info. We gotta keep in touch at least." Jesse started patting himself down in search of something to write on. He came up empty.

Amp handed Jesse a piece of paper and a pen from behind the counter. Jesse wrote his number on it and handed it back to Amp.

"For real, man, keep in touch," Jesse said.

"Of course, man." Amp folded the paper and stuck it in his wallet. "We can grab lunch or something and catch up on my off day."

"Bet."

Jesse paid Amp for the blunts. They dapped each other, and Amp watched Jesse walk out of the store and climb into his SUV.

A part of Amp wanted so badly to run and get in that truck with Jesse and do what he needed to do so that someday—hopefully soon—he could be driving his own ride. It wouldn't have to be a tricked-out vehicle like Jesse's, but it would beat walking. The other part of him knew that his freedom was a whole lot more important than a car. Anyway, Amp had never been big on material things, and the dope game had never been part of Amp's life. He'd always made his money legit, although he'd witnessed first-hand how quickly one could come up slinging drugs. It wouldn't take nearly as long as it would sweeping up a corner store, that's for sure.

He looked around the store as if contemplating doing just that, leaving this stocking shelves business behind for the next cat to tend to. Then, shaking his head, he walked from behind the counter and went back to work. He was going to ride this journey out. No shortcuts. He'd met enough criminals in jail to know that sometimes shortcuts land a person nowhere—dead, or in jail, just that much faster.

Chapter 7

Later on that night, after finishing up at the store, Amp was walking back to the place he called home. His pace slowed when he noticed a police car, with its lights flashing, sitting in the driveway at the halfway house. He wondered whether the police were bringing someone or taking someone away. Either way, it probably wasn't a good thing.

The car was empty and there was no one in sight, but as he stepped into the front yard, he could hear voices coming from inside the house. The screen door flew open, knocking over one of the plastic chairs on the porch, and Amp stopped in his tracks.

"This ain't right!"

Amp watched as two cops wrestled a handcuffed Melvin out of the house, past Mr. Barrett, who stood in the doorway observing the arrest, then toward the waiting cop car. Mr. Barrett followed the officers and Melvin down the steps.

Paul stood on the porch watching everything go down from that viewpoint.

"Come on, man. Just give me one more chance," Melvin pleaded to Mr. Barrett as one of the cops opened the back door of the cruiser.

Mr. Barrett didn't say a word. The smug look on his face made it apparent that he had no intention of giving Melvin another chance. As a matter of fact, the way he looked, Amp suspected he was getting some sort of satisfaction out of seeing yet another black man being handcuffed and thrown into the back of a police car.

Melvin must have sensed it too, because he turned his attention to Paul.

"Mr. Harold! Mr. Harold! You can vouch for me," Melvin said before the officers closed him up in the vehicle.

Brad stuck his head out the front door. "This is some bullshit!" he said to no one in particular.

With a raised eyebrow, Paul turned around and said to Brad, "You wanna go with him?"

"No!" Brad replied without hesitation.

"Then get your goofy ass back in the house."

Brad shook his head in dismay but did as he was told. Amp walked toward the porch to follow suit.

"Hold on. I want you to see this," Mr. Barrett said to him, pointing toward Melvin still pleading in the back of the police car while the officers got into the front seat.

"What happened?" Amp asked.

"Failed his drug test. Had weed and alcohol in his system." Mr. Barrett's answer seemed dry and rehearsed.

"Damn," Amp said under his breath.

"I hope it was worth it." Mr. Barrett shot Amp a disgusted look and then headed to his car and drove off.

Dude enjoys that part of his job way too much, Amp thought as a slight chill ran through his body.

Amp headed up the steps to stand by Paul as they watched the police car take Melvin away.

"Like I said," Paul stated, not taking his eyes off the squad car, "all you guys have to do is follow the rules. Keep your nose clean, do what you need to do to provide for yourself, and then you're on your own. No strings attached. No having to deal with me, and no Mr. Barrett." He shook his head and walked away, leaving Amp standing there, taking in his words and all that he had just witnessed.

Amp's first impression of Mr. Barrett remained the same. His perception of Paul, on the other hand, was changing. At first he hadn't been sure how to read Paul, but now he could see that he was just a decent guy doing his job. All Paul wanted was to see the men in the house doing what they were supposed to do as well.

Paul made it sound easy, and perhaps for some it was, but for guys like Melvin, obviously it was easier said than done. Although Amp was bound and determined to do the right thing, he hoped Melvin's fate wouldn't be his.

The next morning after breakfast and getting his morning workout on, Amp returned to the home, which was permeated with a somber mood. Shit got real last night, and it was just the kind of reminder Amp needed to keep him focused on keeping a job and finishing his ninety days in the house.

Noticing the computer was free, Amp sat down and logged on. The computer wasn't anything fancy or high-tech. It definitely wasn't one of those new twenty-four inch, full HD, flat touchscreen monitors. It was just a regular desktop PC with a monitor and hard drive unit, but that's all Amp needed to do what he had to do.

Amp surfed the Net for a few minutes. He was in the middle of jotting down some information when Paul entered the living room.

Looking over his shoulder instinctively upon feeling the presence of someone else in the room, Amp said, "Paul, what if I want to get a second job?"

Paul's eyes narrowed. "For what?"

"I want to finish my degree." After seeing Melvin arrested last night, Amp had lain in bed and thought about his life before prison. He'd been in college, headed for success. Not for a second had he foreseen prison in his path, but it had only taken one second, one mistake, to change the course of his life. Perhaps, he thought, it wasn't too late to get back on that right path and go back to school.

"These college classes I'm checking out on-line are expensive as hell." Amp turned and faced Paul. "I figure I can get another job and stack my money while I'm here. That way I can pay for my classes and have some money to get an apartment when I leave here. Maybe a little piece-of-shit car." Amp had really thought about what Paul said to him on the porch the previous night as they watched Melvin being driven right back to jail before he ever got a chance at real freedom.

"I don't see anything wrong with it."

Amp turned back to face the computer, but then something else crossed his mind. He turned back around to Paul and asked, "Will Mr. Barrett?"

"I run this over here," Paul was quick to say with authority. "What I say goes. As long as you obey the rules, he has nothing to say about it."

Amp nodded his understanding as he turned back around to face the computer. Staring at the computer screen, he asked another question. "What if it's at a nightclub, doing security or something, with late hours?"

Paul sucked his teeth and was quiet for a moment. It was obvious that he wasn't too sure about the whole nightclub thing. "Well . . . I guess, as long as I can verify the employment and talk with the owner. If everything is legit, maybe. But remember, your parole has been sanctioned as 'no alcohol,' so if you have so much as one drink, you'll be going back to jail. Do you really want that kind of temptation on a daily basis? This may not be a wise decision, Amp."

Amp swung his body around in the chair, turning toward Paul and looking him straight in the eye. "You said you read my file."

"I did."

"Then you know that the last thing I ever wanna do is have another drink. Ever!"

Paul eased up, seeing that he had hit a sensitive subject with Amp. "Just get me the information."

"Thanks, 'cause I'm gonna go check this one place out after I get off at Mr. Lam's tonight," Amp said, taking out his wallet and then pulling out Madam's business card. "But don't worry. I'll make curfew." Amp wanted to clarify that he wasn't running game.

"Okay. Just let me know," Paul said then walked away.

Amp picked up the phone and dialed the number on the business card. It was time to start making power moves and putting some things in place.

Chapter 8

After being on the bus for only a hot second, Amp noticed the address numbers were getting close to where he needed to be. He stood up and signaled to be let off the bus. Had he known that the club was only a mile and a half away from the halfway house, he would have walked.

Stepping out into the evening air, he watched as the Metro took off roaring down La Cienega Boulevard. He looked down at the address on the business card he held in his hand, then at the numbers on the surrounding buildings. He determined that he only needed to walk a bit farther south to find the place. Sure enough, a block later he heard the muffled bass thumping from one of the buildings, and he knew he was getting close. Unless someone was having one hell of a house party in the middle of the week, the music couldn't have been coming from anywhere else but a club.

Within a few more yards, Amp spotted the sign for Club Eden. Bright red light bulbs spelled out each letter. A smaller sign with similar red bulbs spelled out LADIES NIGHT on the wall next to the entrance.

Exactly what kind of club was this? Before going to prison, Amp had been more of a ladies' man, so he was no stranger to clubs of all types, but it had been a while, and he knew the club scene had changed. It always does. He spotted the same customized Aston Martin that he'd seen Madam get into at the park. It was in a reserved space near the front.

As Amp took a good look at the tan stucco building, he thought he remembered the place. Back in the day, this building had been one of the biggest and hottest sports bars in town. It wasn't his regular stomping ground or anything like that, but he'd come over this way before from Long Beach, where he was raised. If this was the same building he was thinking of, he'd been there a couple of times to watch a football and basketball game or two. Come to think of it, this was the place where he'd had one of his first beers. Actually, one night he'd had one beer too many and gotten sick. That was also the last time he'd visited the place. His boys had clowned him good.

The memories of the good old days were making Amp smile, something he hadn't done a lot of in prison. It actually felt somewhat weird to him, so he stopped smiling and redirected his focus on the task at hand.

Amp approached the entrance to see what this place was now. He stepped through the red metal door, and his eyes had to adjust in the darkened foyer. The walls in the entryway were painted black, and the chandelier with ruby red lights was definitely more for show than for seeing. Gold poles with red velvet rope marked the area where people were supposed to line up to enter. The club had a scent to it—not a bad scent, but one Amp couldn't immediately recognize.

Amp spotted the coat check area to the right, and he smiled at the cute little brown-skinned woman who was working there. She returned his look with a friendly smile of her own. There was just something about that chocolate. . . . He thought about how sweet it would be to take her into that coat check room and caress the nape of her neck while he kissed her passionately. After all, it had been a long time in prison, and the feeling of a woman's warmth was well overdue.

He snapped back out of his daydream and regained his focus. He was there for a purpose. Opposite the coat check was a split door with the top half open. The woman sitting behind it was there to admit patrons, but instead she was messing around on her cell phone. There was a sign hanging on the top half of the door listing the entrance fee, which Amp thought was shockingly high. There was another sign that listed a few rules, which Amp didn't bother reading.

"Excuse me," Amp said, but the woman apparently couldn't hear him over the music coming down the short hallway that probably led to the main part of the club. The woman on her phone wasn't paying Amp any mind.

Figuring he'd have to find Madam himself, Amp walked by, down the black marble swirl path. At the end of the hallway, he was taken aback by how much the place had changed since its days as a sports bar. Straight ahead was a stage about ten feet long. The floor was decorated with the same black marble swirl flooring as the foyer. Surrounding the stage were about a hundred anxious-looking, cackling women of all shapes, sizes, and colors. Most of them had some fruity-looking signature drink sitting in front of them. The women were working their crowns of glory, with thousands of dollars' worth of hairstyles done up to perfection: weaves of the highest quality, natural coils, sisterlocks, and dreads. Their faces were beat and their hair was laid. You couldn't tell them that they weren't fierce.

"All right, all right. This is DJ Dime, your voice of reason to keep all you lovely ladies from going insane over what Club Eden's got going on in here tonight."

The women reacted to her announcement. Their chants, hollering, and applause made the place sound as rowdy as a basketball playoff game.

Amp looked around, trying to see who owned the jazzy voice with a hint of sultriness, but he hadn't stepped far enough into the club to be in view of the DJ booth in the back corner of the room.

"Dim the lights in this place. And, ladies, I want all eyes on the spotlight. Give it up for the one, the only, Babyface."

On cue the lights lowered and a spotlight hit the stage. From behind the opening of the dark red velvet curtains appeared a muscular, caramel-skinned man. The diamond in his left ear was sparkling in the light. Standing around six feet tall, the oiled-up gentleman struck a pose, running a hand down his tight haircut. The ladies were whooping and hollering like he was a Greek god or something. He looked like a 23-year-old in the face, but there was no mistaking, from these grown women's reaction, that they sure thought he was all man.

The women were fanning themselves, reaching for him, whistling, and screaming his name. There seemed to be no embarrassment, and certainly no shame. This was their world. Babyface might have been center stage, but these women were definitely the real stars of the show. It was all about pleasing them.

Amp figured out quickly that everything he'd seen so far—from the updated black-and-red décor to the come-hither look Babyface was giving the crowd—was designed to make these ladies feel beautiful. When Babyface locked eyes with a sister in the front row, Amp imagined she probably felt like she was the only woman in the room, and that every muscle he moved was to please her and only her. Unlike its former sports bar atmosphere, now it was a place where every patron was meant to feel sexy and desired. If their men at home hadn't noticed the new hairdo or that new pair of shoes, not to worry. Tonight, they would be noticed.

Amp watched a pair of red lace panties sail through the air and land at Babyface's feet, and now Amp could place the scent he'd noticed when he first walked in. It was lust. Amp shook his head in disbelief. He'd heard of such scenarios at rock concerts or whatnot, but this was the first time he was witnessing it live. These women were out of their minds with lust. The dancers at Club Eden were rock stars in their own right.

As the DJ played "Boots On" by Christian Keyes, Babyface began to dance to the sensual beat. When the artist crooned, "I know how to move to make you hot," Babyface thrust his hips forward, and the women in the crowd went crazy. Babyface then started crawling closer to the end of the stage so that all of the ladies could get a better view as he moved his pelvis up and down, slowly and deeply, to the music. It seemed as if the women were in a trance, until he started gyrating faster and faster. Then it didn't take long for them to start going into their purses and bras, pulling out bills and carpeting the stage with them. Dollars went flying until almost the entire stage was covered. Clearly red was the theme of the club, but green was the favorite color.

Amp stepped farther into the club, still shaking his head in amazement at the level of arousal that had these women coming off of so much money just to enter the club, and then throwing even more on the stage. He wanted to learn more, so he headed toward the bar, hoping the bartender could lead him to Madam.

As he walked over, a thought suddenly came to his mind. He looked back at the stage, where Babyface now had a woman wrapped around his waist. He was thrusting, and she was hanging on tight, like she was riding one of those mechanical bulls.

Could that be the kind of job Madam had in mind for Amp to do? He suddenly remembered the way she had been giving him the once over at the park. When he didn't know what kind of a club it was, he'd assumed she was talking about a job as a bouncer, or maybe just cleaning up the place; but after seeing what went on in Club Eden, he was thinking she might have meant something totally different. Had she been sizing him up, not to see if he could carry a mop and a bucket, but to see if he could bust a move?

"Oh, hell no!" Amp turned around, set on making a beeline toward the exit. It was very possible that he and Madam had two different ideas of work, and he felt no need to hang around and find out the possibilities.

Amp rushed through the foyer, past the woman still playing on her cell phone. He was halfway through the parking lot before he heard someone calling his name.

"Amp?"

He turned around and saw Madam.

"It is Amp, right?" She was wearing an olive-colored satin top, and her cream-colored pencil skirt looked like it was sewn on to fit only her body. She approached him confidently in her ankle-strap pumps.

"Uh, yes. That's right," Amp said, feeling a little awkward. Witnessing her style and class again, he suddenly felt silly for rushing out of the club the way he did. She was probably going to think he was crazy for coming there at all if he wasn't willing to at least hear her out.

Madam's heels clicked on the concrete as she stepped up to Amp. "Leaving so soon?"

"Yeah. I came to see about working for you, but this"—Amp nodded toward the club—"is not my type of party."

"Well, I was thinking along the lines of having you work the front door as security." Madam placed her hand on Amp's shoulder. "You look like you can handle yourself." She gave him the same type of once over that she'd given him at the park, sizing him up, confirming her initial intuition.

"What would I be securing?" Amp asked. "There's only women in there. Mr. Babyface looks like he can handle them just fine." Amp was dead serious.

"You'd be surprised how wild those women can get, especially after a couple drinks. They tend to throw caution to the wind."

"Along with an occasional pair of panties?" Amp added.

"Yeah, that too," she said with a sly smile. She widened her eyes, silently asking Amp to consider the offer. "So, interested?"

He was relieved to hear that she wasn't asking him to gyrate up on that stage the way he'd seen Babyface doing. And he sure could use some extra money to get him closer to his goals of college and a place of his own. If it really was as easy as keeping a few horny sisters in line, he couldn't help but consider the opportunity Madam was presenting to him.

"What's the hours and the pay?" Amp asked.

"Thursday through Sunday, ten-thirty p.m. to two-thirty a.m. Fifteen dollars an hour, plus tips."

Two hundred forty dollars a week would be good, no doubt, but something wasn't adding up, and it made him suspicious. "Wait . . . tips? For being security? Who tips security?"

"Trust me." Madam smiled while eyeballing Amp's physique. "These women are going to like you." She not-so-subtly leaned around to check out his backside. "When can you start?" she asked confidently. She was definitely a woman about her business.

But was it all too good to be true? Amp's doubts were front and center. "I don't know." He needed a minute to take it all in, but he didn't want to waste her time with his indecisiveness either.

Madam rolled her eyes in her head. Clearly she thought Amp was taking too long to make up his mind. When Amp still didn't answer, she shrugged, gave Amp a look that said *you win some you lose some*, and turned to walk away. With every step she took, Amp saw his goals drifting further out of reach.

When he thought of it in those terms, working the door didn't sound so bad. What harm could there be in calming down a rowdy chick or two every now and again?

He was close to accepting the offer, but there was one more thing he felt he needed to say. "Wait," he called out to her.

Madam stopped and turned back around to face Amp.

"Look, I'm in a halfway house," he said.

Her face didn't reveal any feelings about what Amp had just said.

He continued. "I'm on parole. If the supervisor of the house approves it, I can start tomorrow. That's if the offer still stands."

A satisfied smile came across Madam's face. "Have him call me tomorrow."

"Will do." Amp turned to head back to the house, deciding he'd walk this time instead of catching the bus. He had a lot to think about.

"Hey." Madam stopped him. "If you have time, I can show you around."

Amp thought about curfew, but it was only quarter to ten. He still had time for a quick tour. "Okay," he agreed, walking over and extending his elbow for Madam to hold. He had done a li'l time, but he still had all the charms of a true gentleman.

Madam looped her arm through his, reaching her other hand up to give his bicep a quick squeeze. "Oh, yes," she said. "The ladies are definitely going to like you . . . a lot."

Madam and Amp walked back inside, passing the stage on their way to her office. By now the women were being entertained by another dancer, and the room had a whole new energy. They were really hyped up. Amp could see where security might come into play on some occasions.

Amp heard the voice of reason, DJ Dime, chime in over the music. He still hadn't gotten a look at the woman behind the voice, but there was something about her sound that he liked.

"Any of you ladies feeling a little bit under the weather tonight?" DJ Dime asked. "Well, your healing is on the way. Let me introduce to you Dr. Feelgood, 'cause even if he's bad, it's gon' be good."

The women roared, and dollars went flying everywhere. The tall and sexy, chiseled man who took the stage didn't even have to move one of his many muscles before the women were going into their purses. He had eyes that looked right into their lustful souls.

Amp and Madam went into the office, and even with the door closed, Amp could hear that things were cranking up out there. He might need to get started on the job ASAP.

The next morning, Amp was back in his room at the halfway house, standing in front of the open drawer at the top of his dresser. Once again, he was looking at the pictures he'd pulled out of the envelope he kept in there. He knew he had made a lot of strides since he left prison, but there was one great act he still had to accomplish: finding and facing Shannon Ellis. Looking at those photos gave him the motivation he needed to keep moving forward toward his goals.

Amp heard a knock at the door and quickly stuffed the pictures back into the drawer. "Come in," he called out, turning around to realize that his door was cracked and Paul had probably already seen him staring at the photos. Either way, as Amp closed the drawer, Paul said nothing about it.

"I just finished talking to Mary," Paul said, entering the room. "We did a Skype call so she could show me that the club was real, the setup and all that." He'd told Amp he wanted to double-check the legitimacy of this Club Eden. Mr. Lam's corner store he'd been familiar with; Club Eden, not so much. "Not that I can't pop in and see for myself," he warned. "It's a bar, so . . ."

Amp put his hand up to stop Paul. "I know what you're going to say about the alcohol."

"I ain't saying shit. You already know."

Amp let out a deep sigh. How much clearer did he have to make it that he wasn't thinking about putting any alcohol into his body? He would never again jeopardize someone else's life by being under the influence. Period.

He moved on to something else. "Did she tell you about the hours?"

"Yes. That means that if you're off at two-thirty, you can be back here by three. Walking, waiting on a taxi or a bus, it's a short distance. I cleared it with the board, but you must be in this house by three. No exceptions."

Amp was getting used to Paul's repetitive communication style and knew by keeping his answers brief, he could help the conversation end. "Yes, sir."

"I will be calling randomly. You better be there."

"Okay," Amp said, not even worried. He didn't know how many times he had to express that he wasn't going to mess this up. At this point he figured he could show Paul better than he could tell him.

"And you're still going to be responsible for any morning chores you have."

"No problem." Amp was determined to do whatever it took to get his life back in order, like it had been before he went to jail.

Before he messed it all up, Amp had been going to college part-time to study business. He had aspirations of owning and running his own barber shop one day. It wasn't going to be the average establishment. This one was going to be the next best thing to chilling in a bar. He'd have four chairs on each side, with accompanying custom mirrors. A couple of forty-two-inch televisions posted up on the walls would be playing ESPN. In the back, with a brown leather

sectional and matching chairs, would be a
60-inch flat screen with surround sound for
the Lakers games. Since L.A. was the only city
that Amp had known, it was no surprise that
he was a huge Lakers fan. He couldn't wait to
have the best Lakers viewing parties at the shop
while edging the guys up. He could hear the
shit-talking and imagine the camaraderie—all
good moments. The sadness of his past would be
a fleeting memory.

He'd even have a bar, but he wouldn't sell
alcohol, of course. Pre jail, Amp had been a bit
of a drinker, but no more. The bar would be
just for show. It would be placed about four feet
from the stripper pole—now that wouldn't be for
show. The décor would be real suave, an escape
for the fellas.

Amp had been bound and determined to
make it all a reality. In order to fund both his
dream and his education, Amp was cutting hair
on the side—that is, when he wasn't handling
baggage at the airport full-time. It was a step
above being a garbage man, but it was legal.
Plus, Amp didn't mind putting in the hard work
he knew it would take to see his dream mani-
fested.

Half of his friends had illegal hustles going.
Amp didn't want any part of that. He would

still hang out and party with those cats, but that was it. Even so, it was the partying that got him off track. One night and one decision is what ultimately tore his life apart. The day he got locked up, his vision of becoming an entrepreneur began to evaporate, and his dream felt less possible day by day. Now he stood here at ground zero trying to resurrect it.

As if he sensed Amp's intentions, Paul said, "I got a safe here in the house if you want to start putting your money up. That way you don't have to worry about one of these knuckleheads stealing it."

"Cool. Thanks."

Paul walked out of the room, and Amp lay down on his bed, thinking of the future he was determined to reclaim. It was time to get his life back and make his dreams come true.

Chapter 9

"You check the IDs. The girl at the counter will take their money and check their purses," Madam explained to Amp as they stood outside at the club entrance. She always spoke with such passion and concern when it came to her business. Amp could see it in her face; her dedication to the club and her staff was undeniable. She had no children biologically, but this club was her baby indeed.

Amp had been told by one of the gossiping bartenders the story of how Madam started the club. About three years earlier, she was managing the hottest nightclub in town. She booked talent, celebrity hosts, and even came up with the idea to bring in male dancers to put on shows after regular club hours. It became known as the infamous Ladies Night. Madam recruited some of the hottest and most popular dancers from around the map. It didn't take long for the reputation of Ladies Night to spread across the map either.

The nightclub was making money by the box thanks to Madam's savvy ideas. The owner never fought Madam on her ideas and suggestions, because he knew she had the golden touch. Whatever she put into place always seemed to make sense—because it made money. The only problem was that the owner wasn't sharing the wealth. Greed got a hold of him to the point where Madam was barely even getting a cut from the money they made each week from Ladies Night, even though she was booking the talent and handling everything.

Eventually, Madam got fed up and quit the club, convincing the dancers to follow her. Unfortunately, she no longer had a roof for them to perform under. So, she took every dime she had and bought the building that was now the home of Club Eden. She was reaping the full benefits of her business ideas, which were a proven success. Ever since, Madam had been married to Club Eden, which left no time for relationships.

At one point in time, though, there'd been a man by the name of Marcus Clancy who had captured Madam's interest. She was dating him while she managed the other club. They were not quite in love at the time, but they were serious about each other. As Madam dedicated more and more time and committed more of herself to the success of the club, however, Marcus felt a distance growing between them.

It was no secret that Marcus had an issue with Madam being around male strippers with young, hard bodies every day. It wasn't that he couldn't trust Madam, he said; it was those half naked men he didn't trust. Being all about her business, however, Madam wasn't about to give it up just because Marcus was insecure.

Eventually the tension caused them to split up. The bartender said everyone at work knew she must have been hurting, but she hid her emotions, burying herself even deeper into her work. To this day, she had not had another relationship.

As she stood there instructing Amp on his new duties, he could see the fire burning in her. He could understand why her passion for her club left little room for anything else.

"Every fifteen minutes I want you to look inside and make sure everything is cool," Madam continued. "And every half-hour, do a lap around this side of the building." She pointed to her left. "Don't worry about the other side," she said, nodding to her right.

"There's another side to this place?" Last night when Madam showed Amp around, she had introduced him to the staff and told him a little bit about what his duties would consist of. She hadn't shown him, nor mentioned anything about, another side to Club Eden.

"Yes, but that's not your concern."

"Okay," Amp said simply. He knew better than to press for details that she clearly didn't want to give up.

"Come see me at the end of each shift and I'll take care of your pay. Fifteen dollars an hour, as we discussed, and sometimes a little extra, depending on how good the night was. The more money this place makes, the happier I am. The happier I am, the nicer I am with giving out bonuses," she explained.

Amp had no complaints about that, and he had no questions. All of Madam's instructions were pretty clear cut. He nodded in agreement, and Madam walked back into the building.

Over the course of the night, in doing his laps and casing out the place, Amp was amazed by the number of women he saw coming and going. Madam had herself one hell of a business here.

"Can I check your ID please?" Amp asked, stopping a woman and her two friends at the door.

"Damn!" the obviously bold one said, snapping her neck back and checking Amp out. "You can

check whatever you want with your fine ass."
She pulled out her ID and handed it to Amp.
"And that is a current address, just in case you
were wondering."

Her girlfriends laughed in the background as
they pulled out their IDs.

Amp smiled politely but kept his mouth shut.
If he learned anything in jail it was that the less
attention he received, the better. If folks didn't
even notice you were there, then they left you
the hell alone. He had a job to do, and he didn't
want to jeopardize his job by fraternizing with
the customers. Better to smile and act like he
didn't even notice she was flirting.

"Girl, get on out the way," one of her friends
said, bumping her aside as soon as Amp had
checked her ID and handed it back to her.

Amp maintained his professional demeanor,
checking everyone's IDs and moving them along.
"Y'all enjoy yourselves, ladies."

"Oh, we will," the bold one hollered back at
him as they went inside.

No sooner than that trio had made it inside
the club, another pair of women walked up. Amp
held out his hand.

The taller woman opened her purse to get a
twenty, which she put in the palm of his hand.

"Oh no, ma'am. You pay inside," Amp said, trying to give the money back to her.

"I know that. I'm a regular here. I know how it's done," she said. "That's for you." The woman kept a straight face as she reached down and closed Amp's fingers around the money.

So, this is what Madam meant about tips, he thought.

As he checked the woman's ID, he could feel her eyes burning a hole through him. She ran her tongue across her top lip as she checked him out.

"You know, there is way more where that came from." The woman nodded toward the door. "You should be in there on the stage."

Amp looked down at his attire. He wasn't dressed anything like the guys on stage dressed. He was wearing a black V-neck with SECURITY in small white letters on the left side of his chest and in larger letters across his back. The shirt was fitted just enough to see the impression of his well-defined chest, shoulders, and arms pressing through. He had on the same pair of jeans that he'd worn to work at the store. Nothing special, yet these women were tripping over him.

"Thank you for the compliment, ma'am, but I'm right where I'm supposed to be," Amp assured her with much certainty in his tone.

The thought that he could make a lot more money on stage remained in the back of Amp's mind—where it belonged. No way was he going to have the guys in the halfway house knowing he was taking it off for a living. Besides, he could only imagine what Paul would have to say about it.

She shrugged. "Oh, well. Can't blame a girl for trying."

Amp quickly scanned her friend's ID and handed it back to her, and the women went inside to enjoy the night.

All night long women flirted with Amp, and a couple even tucked dollar bills down his shirt. By two o'clock in the morning, most of the patrons had left, but some were still trickling out here and there. When there didn't seem to be anyone else exiting, Amp walked inside the club to check things out. The place was nearly empty. That's when he realized it was already 2:30 a.m. He made a mental note to go to the mall and pick up a watch. Nothing fancy, just something to tell time, to make sure he made it back to the halfway house on time each night.

Amp looked up and saw Madam approaching him with the woman who'd slipped him the twenty spot, and her friend. Amp noticed the taller woman put her hand to her mouth and then lean in to whisper something in Madam's ear.

"Yes, this is Amp," Madam confirmed as they stopped in front of him. Obviously the woman had been whispering about him. "He's the newest family member of Club Eden's security." Madam looked to Amp. "Amp, this is Marla and Veronica." She nodded to the taller lady first and then to her friend. "They're regulars here, so you'll probably be seeing a lot of them."

Amp nodded his second greeting to these particular women for the night.

"And if I'm lucky," Marla said, "perhaps we'll be seeing a lot of you too."

"Down, girl," Madam said to Marla, laughing. "Let me walk you ladies to your car."

As they walked past, Madam lingered a couple steps behind and slipped Amp a wad of cash.

"Thank you," Amp said. "See you tomorrow."

She gave him a quick nod and then caught up to Marla and Veronica.

As Amp stood there counting his money, a sleek and sexy shadow in his peripheral vision caught his attention. He turned to get a better look. It was DJ Dime, standing in the semi-darkened room, packing up her equipment, and damn, she looked every bit as fine as she sounded.

He was enjoying the view when she looked up and caught him. Amp nodded to her, and she nodded back. For a second he thought about going over to talk to her, but then one of the dancers came in and started flirting with her, and Amp figured that was his cue to leave. Besides, it was getting late, and he didn't want to miss his curfew. He walked out the door with his night's pay in his pocket, making him feel like he was one step closer to his goals. That faint glimmer of hope in his eye was back.

"Hey, Sleeping Beauty, time to wake up." Paul had invited himself in the room to discover Amp lying in bed, still in a deep sleep.

Amp thought he heard Paul's voice, but he couldn't get himself to move. All he wanted to do was sleep at least ten more minutes. Paul wasn't going to let that happen.

He shouted, "This ain't summer camp, Amp. Rise and shine!"

Amp shot up straight in the bed. "I'm up. I'm up." He wiped his eyes and focused on Paul, who was looking rather serious this morning.

"Get up. You got chores to do, and you need to drop today," Paul told him, lowering his voice, but not by much.

"Drug test this early?" Amp kicked the covers off and placed his feet on the floor. "Damn."

"Yep, this early." Paul set the sample cup on the nightstand.

Amp grabbed it and headed for the bathroom.

"Leave the door open," Paul said.

Amp gave Paul the side-eye but did as he was told. A couple minutes later, he returned to the bedroom with urine sample in hand. He gave it to Paul.

"Happy?" Amp asked sarcastically.

"Look, I hate this just as much as you do. You think I want to be handling someone's bodily fluids first thing in the morning—or at all, for that matter? But it's got to be done." Paul turned to leave, but not before throwing over his shoulder, "You have a sink full of dishes waiting on you. Handle that."

"I'm on it." Amp sighed, but there was no use in complaining. These were the consequences of past choices he'd made.

Amp headed into the bathroom to get himself together, having no idea of the drama that awaited him later in the day.

Chapter 10

As Amp swept up the store toward closing time, Mr. Lam was behind the counter finishing up some paperwork. He was swaying his head and nodding every now and then to the Asian music that was playing from the mini boom box between the two registers on the counter. From the looks of it, the artist must have been singing about something quite interesting, to Mr. Lam anyway.

"Hey, Mr. Lam, are you ever going to play anything else besides this stuff?" Amp stopped sweeping momentarily.

Picking up the papers and tapping the bottom of the pages on the counter to even them up, Mr. Lam replied, "I'm leaving, so you can play whatever music you want. Just no cursing. Customers no hear that." With papers in hand, Mr. Lam headed to the back office to get his personal belongings. A couple minutes later, he was leaving for the night. "See you tomorrow," he said to Amp as he left the store.

As soon as Amp finished sweeping and put away the broom, a customer came into the store. While the dude walked over to the freezer, Amp made his way behind the counter, prepared to ring up his purchases and then lock up the store.

The customer came over and set a twenty-two ounce beer on the counter. Amp's eyes went from the beer to the lit cigarette in the customer's hand.

"I'm going to need you to put that out, please," Amp said.

The customer paused for a minute, staring at Amp, then he threw the cigarette on the ground and put it out with his foot.

Even though Amp had just finished sweeping the floor, he let it slide. It was near closing time and he didn't want any issues. He was going to encounter assholes for the rest of his life, but it didn't mean he had to react to them. He even refrained from shooting the customer as much as a dirty look, staying focused on the transaction.

"Can I get you anything else?" Amp asked after ringing up the beer and placing it in a brown paper bag.

"Yeah," the customer replied. "You can hit that money button and open the drawer."

"My bad. I didn't hear you." Amp had yet to turn off the Asian music, so he wasn't being funny; he really didn't hear the guy. He couldn't have said what Amp thought he'd heard.

The customer showed Amp his machete, holding it flat across the counter. "You heard me. Hit that money button."

Amps eyes stayed glued on the weapon. "Oh, that button." Amp didn't even think about not hitting that button. He'd been locked up with dudes who'd had no problem using one of those things on somebody, and he was not about to risk his life when he was just getting it back together. He hit the button and opened the drawer. "There's money in that register too." Amp nodded toward the second register. "You want me to hit that button too?" He wanted to keep this dude calm, and he figured the best way to do it was to make it clear he was cooperating. It might not have been proper procedure, but neither was the machete that was staring him in the face. Amp just wanted this all to be over with sooner rather than later.

"Why not?" the guy replied with a shrug.

Amp hit the button on the second register as the robber reached over and emptied out the first one.

"You need a bag to put the money in?" Amp asked.

"That's a good idea."

Amp handed the man a brown paper bag as the robber emptied out the second cash register. With his hands raised in the air, Amp watched silently. He didn't want any problems. "You smoke Kools or Newports?" Amp asked.

The robber looked confused.

"We got cartons of cigarettes back here."

"Newports," he replied, shaking his head. He'd probably never had such a cooperative robbery victim.

"I'm gonna grab you a couple cartons, if that's cool."

The robber said, "I wish all my robberies went this smooth. I had to shoot the last guy."

Amp slowly placed the cartons of Newports on the counter, feeling sure that he'd made the right move by cooperating. If this guy had shot someone, then obviously he was unstable enough to use the machete. Amp backed away, keeping his eyes on the blade. "If you need some cereal and milk for the kids in the morning, it's in aisle two. Whatever you need, help yourself."

"Why you so damn helpful anyway?" The robber started tapping the machete against his leg.

"'Cause I'm not trying to die over no minimum wage job."

"What are you gonna do when I walk out that door?"

"Wait about five or ten minutes then call the cops."

The robber bobbed and weaved his head in an attempt to get Amp to focus on him. It was useless, as Amp kept his eyes on the weapon.

"Why ain't you looking at me?"

"I don't wanna know what you look like. That way you don't have a reason to kill me." Amp turned his head toward the wall, looking in the opposite direction from the man.

The robber didn't respond. As a matter of fact, for the next few seconds Amp didn't hear anything. When a few more seconds had passed, he heard the sound of the door closing. This made him nervous. If another customer was walking in on the robbery, no telling what could happen. After a moment of uninterrupted silence, Amp finally decided to risk a peek at the spot where the robber had been standing. Discovering that the guy had exited the store, Amp hurried over and locked the door, breathing a sigh of relief.

"This is some bullshit here!" he swore. "I was safer in prison."

For the second time since Amp had arrived at the halfway house, a cop car with flashing lights was pulling up into the driveway.

"Damn it. Now what?" Paul said as he walked out onto the porch. He was surprised to see Amp being let out of the back of the car. Of all the guys in the house, Amp was the one he would have least expected to see in this situation. He had gotten a job so fast, and Paul really thought he was on the right track.

Paul stepped off the porch to go ask questions. He went straight to Amp, rather than talking to the cops. After all, LAPD had a reputation—a not so stellar one—and Paul still wanted to give Amp the benefit of the doubt.

"What happened?" he asked Amp.

"I got robbed at the store. I gave them my statement," Amp replied, holding his hands out to show Paul that he wasn't wearing handcuffs. "They ran my name, found out I'm on parole, and brought me here."

A look of relief passed over Paul's face upon hearing that Amp hadn't messed up. He looked toward the two officers who had walked up behind Amp. Introducing himself as the one in charge of the house, he thanked them for bringing Amp back. They nodded, but neither one had much to say. These guys were a little too uptight for Paul's taste.

"Okay then . . ." Paul said, breaking the awkward silence. He looked to Amp. "Well, unless you're too shook up, shouldn't you be headed over to your other job?" Paul looked back to the officers. "That is, if you guys are finished with him."

The officers nodded silently again.

"Yes," Amp replied. "I should get going. I'm gonna go get changed." He hurried into the house without looking back.

Paul looked to the officers. "Thanks again."

One of the officers finally spoke. "No problem. But keep your eye on that one."

Paul looked over his shoulder then back at the officer. "I think that one is going to be just fine. You have a good night, officers," he said then headed back inside.

The next day at the store, a glooming feeling hung in the atmosphere. After the robbery, Mr. Lam had been called back to the store, so he'd been there when Amp gave his story to the cops. This morning, for some reason, he'd already asked Amp to reiterate the story twice. Since the non-working security cameras were just there for show, Mr. Lam had to take Amp's word for how things went down. The fact that Mr. Lam continued to ask questions gave Amp the feeling that his boss was suspicious of his story.

Amp had been on the clock for a couple of hours and was busy stocking beverages into the cooler, wishing there wasn't so much tension in the place. Mr. Lam had gone in the back to take a phone call. Amp looked up to check out the black car with dark-tinted windows just sitting out front in the store parking lot. It had pulled up a few seconds ago, but no one had gotten out. Amp felt his heartbeat speed up. What if it was another robbery getting ready to take place? Amp couldn't imagine coming out of a second robbery unscathed like he had the first one.

He walked toward the front of the store, wondering whether he should lock the door. Just then, Mr. Lam came out from the back.

"I need to talk to you, Amp." Mr. Lam's head was down; he wouldn't even look Amp in the eyes.

"What's up, Mr. Lam?" Amp had a bad feeling in the pit of his stomach, and now it wasn't because of the car outside.

Mr. Lam shook his head, finally making eye contact. "I'm going to have to let you go."

"What?" Amp felt confused and a little pissed off. As far as he was concerned, he'd done a hell of a job in the little bit of time he'd been working there, and had even come close to dying while doing it. "You don't think I had anything to do with that robbery, do you?" All of a sudden it made sense to Amp. Mr. Lam probably had him repeat the story to see if he could catch him in a lie. He probably thought Amp had set everything up with one of his buddies and had benefitted from the robbery.

Mr. Lam shook his head. "It has nothing to do with that," he explained, proving Amp's theory wrong. "I filed my claim for the robbery with the insurance company. They found out from the police report that I have a convicted felon working at my store."

A look of shame slid across Amp's face.

"Sorry. You good worker." Mr. Lam continued. "It's no big deal to me, but they double cost of insurance if I keep you on. I can't afford that." Mr. Lam shot Amp a stern look and wagged his index finger. "Why you not told me?"

"You didn't ask, so I didn't think that it mattered." Amp hadn't been deliberately trying to withhold information from Mr. Lam, but after his experience trying to find a job at the mall, he hadn't been in any hurry to divulge his status as a convict. It was sort of an "If they don't ask, I don't tell" policy.

"Sorry. Nothing I can do." Mr. Lam walked over to the cash register, opened the drawer, and counted out some money. He walked back over to Amp and handed him a wad of bills. "Here's money I owe you for this week."

Amp paused for a moment, trying to conjure up any words that might convince Mr. Lam to change his mind. It was useless, though. Deep down, he knew he would have done the same thing if he were in Mr. Lam's position, so he did not fault him. Without counting it, Amp took the money and put it in his pocket. "Thank you."

Mr. Lam nodded sadly and watched Amp leave.

"Two steps forward, one step back," Amp said to himself as he walked back toward the halfway house with his shoulders slumped and his head hung low. Just as he was getting back on track, some fool with a machete had derailed his plans. The whole situation left a bitter taste in his mouth.

Chapter 11

Babyface stood at the foot of the California king-sized bed in the luxuriously decorated bedroom, pulling up his pants.

"You mean you're really going to leave?" the woman lying in the bed asked. "But we make such good music together. What do you say we spend the day dancing to the beat of our own drum?"

Even with her hair scattered, a couple pieces sweeping across her face, she still looked beautiful. What Babyface couldn't figure out was how in the hell that same sexy red lipstick that covered her pouty lips and had lured him to her home last night was still visible on her lips. Sure, it was a slight pink now, but it was still there, even after all she'd done with that mouth. A chill ran through Babyface's body just thinking about it. *Whoo-wee! She should get a patent on that thing!*

"I wish I could stay, uh . . ." He tried his best to recall her name. The last thing he wanted to do to a woman who knew how to strike a chord on his musical instrument was offend her by not even recalling the songstress's name. Oh, and how she could blow. She'd hit high notes that Babyface had never heard any other woman reach. Whatever her name was, she was definitely an octave above the rest.

"Babydoll," the woman offered, as if she couldn't bear to watch him struggle to remember.

"Excuse me?" Babyface said. Had this woman just called him Babydoll instead of Babyface?

"You can call me Babydoll," she told him. "Get it? Babyface"—She pointed to him—"and Babydoll." She pointed to herself.

Clearly Babyface had given her his name and she'd remembered it. That made him feel even more embarrassed. Caught up in her lustful web, at least he'd remembered to give her his dance name instead of his given name. He never knew what type of chick he'd be dealing with by the end of the night, so just like how some women gave out their middle name instead of their first when they weren't sure about a dude, his dancer name came in handy for that same purpose.

"Oh, what a great duet we make, wouldn't you say?" Babydoll didn't speak her words. She

cooed them in a sexy mixture between Toni
Braxton's singing voice and speaking voice.

He nodded. "Yes, we do . . . Babydoll." Spotting
his socks, Babyface scooped them up and then
sat on the olive green bench at the foot of the
bed, his back now toward Babydoll. "But I have
to go. Trust me, sweetheart, when I say there is
nowhere else on earth I'd rather be."

"Really?" she purred.

Babyface paused just long enough to look into
her big, dark brown eyes that actually reminded
him of a baby doll. It was those eyes that had him
frozen like a deer in headlights from the moment
he'd seen her. Well, those eyes and those legs.

On his way home after dancing at the club last
night, Babyface had stopped at the gas station.
Fortunately, that last little bit of gas in his car
had gotten him to the gas station before the tank
ran dry. He soon discovered that his luck was
truly just starting to unfold when he watched
a red sports car pull up and then a pair of long,
sexy legs step out of it.

Dressed in a pair of shorts with a tank top, the
woman proceeded to strut over to the pump in
her four-inch heels, swinging her hips as if she
knew he was watching her. As she swiped her
credit card at the pump, Babyface looked in her
car at the passenger's side. Surely, if a man had

been accompanying this beauty, he wouldn't be allowing her to pump her own gas. Happy to see that she was in fact alone, Babyface offered to pump her gas. She declined at first, but he insisted. She was playing hard to get, and her sexy antics were working like a charm.

This chick was a bold one. Babyface could feel her standing there, leaned up against her car like she owned the entire gas station, staring him down. Even when he looked up and caught her staring, she didn't blush or try to turn the other way. She obviously wanted there to be no doubt that she liked what she saw.

Afterward, she insisted on thanking Babyface for his act of chivalry, and she had—real good, at least three times—which was why he was now in the bedroom at her house.

"I understand you have to go," Babydoll said, "but before you do, can I get one last dance?"

Babyface heard some movement behind him. He looked over his shoulder and watched as the naked woman underneath the sheets reached over and pressed the button on her CD player. The long arch of her back and a single butt cheek peeking out from underneath the sheets as she reached over had Babyface mesmerized. Suddenly his last concern was getting those socks on his feet; he was more interested in getting another condom on, so they could go for another round.

Some old classic R. Kelly came on and the sheets came off. There she lay, in all of her womanly glory, both sets of lips smiling at him, beckoning him to let the music play. She raised up on her elbows, bending her knees and holding them open, unashamed and unembarrassed. She knew what she was working with and was proud of it. The Brazilian wax was definitely worth showing off. Babydoll just knew she was irresistible.

"I'm sure you call yourself Babyface for lots of reasons," Babydoll murmured, "but, baby, right about now I know where I want that pretty little face of yours." She bit her bottom lip and flung her head back, raising her finger to beckon Babyface to her.

He began to move toward her while undoing his pants. "You sure you can handle another round?" he asked.

"I hear you talking." She lifted her head and looked him dead in the eyes. "So put your money where your mouth is—or your tongue anyway."

"Be careful what you ask for, Babydoll. You just might get it."

He climbed in between her legs, and within seconds her head was thrown back in ecstasy.

It didn't take long before she was hitting those same notes she'd hit last night, as he used his tongue to kill her softly with the song he was playing on her clit.

Babydoll moaned as he pressed his tongue hard against her magic spot. She twisted, turned, and squirmed, trying not to lose control. When he buried his tongue as far inside her walls as it could go, she squeezed her knees together just a little too hard, putting Babyface in a headlock. Her mind was on the beautiful sensation going on between her legs; she forgot that it was Babyface's head between her legs causing the feeling.

Babyface pushed her thighs apart as he continued to flick his tongue on her clit at a rapid speed. She could no longer control herself, as she lifted her waist up off the bed, rolling her hips gently, feeding herself to Babyface.

"Oh, Babyface," she said. "Baby, baby . . ." She began to tremble and pump herself against his mouth. "Encore," she cried out after her sweet melody dripped from her precious part. She rested herself back down on the bed and exhaled, so relaxed that she could have just curled up and fallen off to sleep.

"Oh, no you don't." Babyface came up from between her legs. "Not after what I just did. You better get on over here and handle this."

Babydoll was not one to back down from a challenge. She sat up and pushed him back, her long, painted nail jabbing into the flesh of his chest. It hurt so good.

She slid his pants down and climbed on top, kissing him all over his chest, tracing the trail her lipstick had left from the first time she'd traveled that path. Her hand had made it to his manhood before her lips, so she stroked him gently, then started teasing his tip with the flickering of her tongue.

Babyface did all that he could to restrain the note he wanted to release. He'd just declared security in being a man, so he wasn't about to go out curling his toes and calling out her name, even if he was damn near close to it as she took in inch after inch after inch.

"You know you want to say my name," Babydoll crooned in between licks. "But that's okay. I'm sure you don't remember it." She giggled and then continued to handle her business.

Babyface couldn't even argue with her. He could hardly remember his own name.

Up and down her mouth went on his vessel as she played with his balls with her free hand. Thank goodness this woman couldn't see him biting down on his bottom lip in order to lock in his vocals. It felt so good it hurt! He gripped the sheet as he exploded in ecstasy.

She kept going after he came, when his manhood was extremely sensitive, and he couldn't help but moan loudly.

She sat up on her knees with a look of victory on her face, but Babyface wasn't about to let her think for one minute that she'd won the battle. He'd figured out last night that she loved being manhandled, so he raised up and flipped her over forcefully. Her satisfied smile let him know that she liked that shit.

Babyface put another condom on and entered her from behind. "Scandalous" by Prince came on—the perfect song for the moment.

"You real slick with that mouth," Babyface said as he entered her from the back. "So I think it's time for you to get a spanking." As Babyface moved in and out of her, he smacked her sexy chocolate ass. Between the sound of their skin slapping together and his hand slapping her ass, they were both going crazy, and it didn't take long for them to begin moaning in unison as they climaxed.

"Oh, shit." Babyface rolled over onto his back, out of breath.

"Oh my God, that was sooooo good," Babydoll said as she rested her head on his sweaty chest. She felt like she had been baptized in his sweat, but she didn't mind.

If you're not sweating, you're not doing it right, she thought.

Babyface smiled proudly. He knew he had strung her violin just right, plucking in all the right spots. "Yes, it was. We make beautiful music indeed," Babyface said as the two lay there, eyes closed, marinating in the lingering lust.

"I'm going to have to be a bad girl more often if that's the kind of punishment I have in store." She rubbed her hand up and down his chest.

"I like the sound of that," Babyface said as he twisted a dampened strand of her hair around his finger. Eventually they were making a whole different kind of music: a chorus of *Z*'s and slow, heavy breathing.

Babyface's eyes shot open and immediately landed on the clock, which read 9:59.

"It's morning already," he said, somewhat dazed. Feeling the weight on his chest, he looked down and spotted a sleeping Babydoll. He glanced over toward the window, where he saw no sign of the sun that had been shining before he closed his eyes, which felt like only minutes ago. Babyface closed his eyes again, but then reality set in.

"Oh, shit!" He moved Babyface's head off his chest and jumped out of the bed.

Babydoll opened her eyes. "What's wrong?" she asked groggily.

"It's ten o'clock. That's what's wrong." Babyface had put his pants on, and was hopping around on one foot as he tried to slip a sock on the other one. "I gotta get to work."

"Call off," she said nonchalantly as she fell backward. "And get your fine ass back in this bed."

"I wish I could," he said, now putting on his other sock. "But I can't." He spotted his shirt and slipped it over his head. "I have to get to work. I'm late. It'll be my second time this week." He picked up his shoes, opting not to sit down and put them on, but to carry them with him and put them on in the car. "Sorry, but I've gotta go." He exited the room.

Then, just as quick, he poked his head back in and said, "My boss is going to have my ass." He blew her a kiss and then ran off again.

Babydoll pulled the cover up to her neck. "She can have your ass." She smiled wickedly. "But I had it first."

Chapter 12

Amp tried to keep his head up later on that evening while he put in his work at Club Eden, but the setback of losing his job taunted his thoughts. He was thinking about it as he checked the perimeter of the parking lot. As he rounded the corner of the building to check the back, he saw a car speeding away. There was no one going in to the dancers' entrance, so whoever was driving the car hadn't been dropping off someone. Distracted by his own messed-up situation, Amp did a quick check of the back, saw that nothing looked suspicious, and headed back to his post at the front door without another thought about the car.

Standing by the front door, he pulled out his wallet and removed the paper with Jesse's number on it. Deep in thought, he considered calling Jesse to put in some work. Why not? Being legit was proving not to pay off, at least not as fast as Amp would have liked it to. On second thought, however, sitting back in prison wouldn't be any better. He'd met more of his share of cats in prison who were there because they, too, felt they could make a quick buck by slinging dope. Some of them were serving more time than dudes who had committed murder. That was not the life for Amp. He placed the piece of paper back in his wallet and tucked his wallet away. For the time being, he would have to be satisfied with the money he was making at the club—and thanks to the generous women who tipped him as they made their way inside, the money wasn't too bad, he decided.

After checking a few IDs, getting flirted with by a couple chicks, and having that lovely US currency slipped into his pocket, Amp stepped away from the door to make sure things were kosher on the inside of Club Eden. Everything appeared to be in order, so he went outside, toward the dancers' entrance in back, to check on things. He saw a red sports car, which he recognized as Babyface's, come barreling into the parking lot.

"I'm late again," Babyface said as he hopped out of the car. "She's about to cuss me out." He rushed by Amp with his duffle bag in tow. "Don't ever be late, new guy."

"I won't. And it's Amp."

Babyface stopped and gave Amp the proper greeting. "My bad. I'm just a little tense. Running late when you're employed by Madam will do that to you." He shrugged. "But heck, I'm going to have to deal with her wrath anyway. No disrespect, Amp. They call me Babyface."

"Good to meet you, bruh." The two shook hands, and Babyface continued. "Madam ain't try to get you to dance?"

"No, but it looks like a bunch of new guys are here tonight," Amp told Babyface. In addition to the female clientele, he'd witnessed a few new male faces coming through the doors as well.

"That's just for amateur night. That's how I got started. Did amateur night a year ago, made four hundred dollars in thirty minutes, and I was hooked. Nothing beats getting so much cold, hard cash in your hand every night. I can't make this kind of money doing anything else—and it's exhilarating to turn on so many women at one time. They just can't get enough. Everybody is winning up in here."

"Four hundred in thirty minutes?" Amp asked. It sounded too good to be true. "So, what could somebody make a week, doing that?" Amp's curiosity was piqued.

"Slow week, a stack. A good week, two to three stacks."

"Damn." Amp rubbed his chin. Now that wasn't no chump change, not for just showing a little skin here and there.

"Yeah. Not bad for four nights of work."

"How do you sign up for amateur night?" Amp asked, suddenly considering a turn on stage. It wasn't like he was thinking about doing this full time, but there was no doubt he was in need of money. After all, this was a hell of a lot better than working for Jesse, which he'd been considering just a short while ago. Amp had even danced once in a similar amateur show, on a drunken dare from a college girlfriend who helped him spend the money he made. At the time he hadn't imagined he'd ever be doing it again, but after meeting Babyface and some of the others, he was starting to figure out that they were pretty much like him—regular dudes trying to get paid. Maybe he could do it, just this once, to make up for what he'd be missing from the store until he could find a second job.

"Sign up at the counter. And not on no funny business, but if you need some pointers, let me know. Oh, and you're going to need to see Madam about getting an outfit."

Amp was quite familiar with the "outfits" the dancers wore. He'd gotten a glimpse of one or two on the occasions he'd gone into the club to check things out. There was Babyface, letting a lady from the audience rub baby oil on him as the oil dripped down his gas station uniform pants. Then there was that thing Dr. Feelgood did with his stethoscope, and that dancer who went by the name El Fuego, with his maracas.

"Bet. I'll holler at you after your shift is over." Amp gave Babyface some dap and then Babyface headed inside while Amp walked back around to the front door.

Amp stood at his post for a couple minutes before a car pulled up. The driver, a fly, young-looking dude in his early twenties got out of the driver's seat. His boys stepped out of the car as well, and all four men headed toward the front door.

"Eric, man, you sure this is the right place?" one of the backseat passengers asked.

"I think this is the spot," the driver answered, not sounding too sure of himself.

"Yo, my man. You prolly want the other side, where the women are. It's all dudes dancing on this side." Amp had learned on his first night working the club that the other side of the club was for male entertainment. Security over there was a whole other ball game. Those dudes were huge—had to be pushing three hundred fifty pounds, if not four hundred. There was an off duty cop who moonlighted as security and carried his weapon. Clearly a rowdy female was easier to handle than a rowdy male.

"Oh, my bad. We high as hell," Eric said. He took a good look at Amp. "Where do I know you from?"

"Nothing personal, but I don't know who you are."

Eric stared at Amp, still trying to figure out where he might know him from. Nothing was registering. Finally he gave up. "You say the chicks are around this way?" he asked.

"Yes, sir."

"Thanks." As Eric and his friends walked around to the other side, he kept looking over his shoulder, insisting to his boys that he knew Amp from somewhere. Amp watched him until he disappeared around the corner just to make sure they made it to the other side without causing any trouble.

Left alone with his own thoughts, Amp's mind wandered back to the possibility of hitting the stage. What if there was something more to this dancing thing than just dancing? He'd heard stories about female dancers who started dancing with the intentions of paying off bills or college tuition. One thing led to another, and they ended up in the business of selling sex. Who's to say that didn't happen with male dancers as well? Nobody, which was why when all was said and done, Amp decided to stick with what he'd been hired to do and pass on the whole amateur night business. There had to be another way.

He finished up the night, went inside, and squared up with Madam over at the bar. Tucking his cash in his pocket, Amp prepared to head out.

There were two women walking behind Amp, and he heard one remark, "I'd end up filing bankruptcy if he ever got up on that stage." Amp could practically see the dollar signs and picture the money flying onto the stage. Was he making the right decision? There was a lot of money passing through this club, and from the women's reactions, he knew he had the innate ability and looks to get it.

He turned around with a smile and struck up a conversation with the two ladies.

Dr. Feelgood, a Caucasian dancer who went by the name of Casanova, and a Latin dancer named El Fuego were all walking out from the dressing room.

"Hey, look. The doorman's getting a little action," El Fuego said. A very well-built Latino with green eyes and a five o'clock shadow, he had been dancing for Madam since she opened the club. He hypnotized and mesmerized the women with his looks and Latin dance techniques, which often involved pulling a lucky woman on stage and making her wet with excitement as he led her through his dance of ecstasy.

Amp heard his smart comment, but ignored it to maintain his professionalism as he continued talking to the ladies.

Dr. Feelgood decided to have his say. "If you ladies tip him, he might frisk you."

As the guys laughed, Babyface and another dancer came walking out to join the group.

Amp turned around and faced the men as the women headed toward the exit, not hanging around to hear the grown men's back and forth banter. "You got a lot of jokes for somebody that's wearing a thong," Amp shot back.

The laughter immediately ceased, as none of the dancers found Amp's comment amusing.

"Oh, he speaks," Dr. Feelgood said, breaking the silence. There were chuckles.

"I do more than that." Amp's face was stoic. He might as well have been back on the yard at that moment. The wrong move by Dr. Feelgood and he was getting a WorldStar–quality ass-wh-upping.

"Hey, ol' boy is all right," Babyface said. "Leave him be."

"That your new BFF or something?" Dr. Feelgood chimed in.

"No, your mom is," Babyface said.

The dancers started laughing and cracking jokes as they walked away, easing the tension.

The piercing screech of tires and a deafening crash woke Amp out of his sleep. He shot straight up in his bed, drenched in sweat, looking around the room in confusion. It took him a few seconds to realize where he was. Just moments ago, he'd been tossing and turning in bed as his mind took him to that dark place, where there seemed to be no light at the end of the tunnel. He lay back down, still breathing heavily as his heart slowed to a normal pace. Amp stared up at the ceiling, willing his eyes to stay open—anything but close them and risk drifting back into that nightmare.

Amp turned his head toward the nightstand. The glow of the clock radio provided just enough light for him to see the newspaper clipping he'd left there. It was like it was taunting him. Asleep or awake, it didn't matter: he could not escape the memories of the accident, thoughts of Shannon and the real-life nightmare he'd caused. Amp closed his eyes and drifted off into another fitful sleep.

The next morning, Amp got up, inhaled breakfast, and made an important phone call. When he heard the voice mail recording, he left a brief message with the number where he could be reached at the halfway house. Next he turned on the computer and typed the name "Patrice Ellis" into the search engine. Opening the desk drawer, he pulled out paper and a pen and copied some information from the screen.

As he was writing, the phone rang. Amp took a second to finish what he was writing, dropped the pen and then answered the phone.

"Hello . . . That was me. I called. It's Amp, from the club. . . . Listen, I need to make a li'l bread. I'm gonna do the amateur night next Wednesday. . . . I'ma see what I can find on YouTube, but I'm still going to need some pointers. . . . I'm free tomorrow during the day. . . . Bet. Thanks, man."

Amp hung up the phone, feeling confident that he was making the right decision, one that would get him back on track. Growing up, he certainly never had ambitions to become a male dancer, but as a grown man now, he did have ambitions to be independent and to go back to school. If one night on stage would get him closer to his mission, then he'd decided he was good with that.

He looked down at the piece of paper where he'd written some information, folded it, and placed it in his pocket.

Paul entered the room, and Amp looked up to greet him. "What's going on?"

"You tell me. What's your plan now that Mr. Lam let you go?"

"Try to pick up some extra hours at the club." Amp paused for a second, not sure whether to share his full plan with Paul. Deciding that honesty was probably the best route to go with Paul, he admitted, "I'm going to . . . do the amateur night over there at the club next week." He continued, intent on defending himself before Paul had a chance to voice his opinion. "I ain't proud of it, but it's a good way to make some money legally." He braced himself for Paul's response.

"Amateur night, as in dancing?"

Amp nodded.

Paul folded his arms thoughtfully. "Hmmm. I'm not sure how I feel about it, but it's really not up to me. Just be careful of the situations you put yourself in. The deeper you get into something like that, the more things you have access to. Bad things." Paul gave Amp a knowing look.

"I hear you. I'm going to try to find another daytime job too, but for now, it's not like anyone is knocking the door down for me to come work for them."

"Okay." Without further comment, Paul walked away, and Amp turned back around to log off of the computer. A photo of Patrice Ellis faded out as the computer shut down.

Amp was standing next to Babyface, who was sitting at the bar with a very sexy woman planted next to him. She had one hand on Babyface's thigh while the other played with the stem of the cherry in her mixed drink. Her scented body lotion, the aroma of fresh fruit, smelled good enough to eat. Judging from the way she was rubbing up on Babyface, that was probably her intent—to be his edible treat.

Amp was trying to fight his nerves as he hit Babyface up for some last-minute advice on his amateur night performance. Two days ago, they had met up, and Babyface shared some moves and techniques with Amp. Everything was pretty basic, but it was enough to get him through tonight's set. Even though Amp had been on a stage once years ago, he'd seen how wild the crowds in Club Eden could get, and his nerves were trying to get the best of him.

"If you don't remember anything else," Babyface said, "remember this: Make them pay you before you start taking shit off." He turned to the woman next to him. "Ain't that right?"

She licked her lips and stared Babyface dead in the eyes as she tucked a hundred dollar bill in the waistband of his pants. Babyface turned and nodded to Amp, proving his point.

Babyface continued. "You got about ten minutes up there, so work the crowd. Pay special attention to the big girls. They pay the best." The bartender placed a glass in front of Babyface, who grabbed it and held it up to Amp. "You need a shot before you go up?"

Amp shook his head. "I don't drink. Thanks."

Shrugging, Babyface threw the shot of Hennessy straight down his throat. The woman sitting with him removed the cherry stem from her mouth. It was neatly tied in a knot. This further enticed Babyface, who cleared his throat and shook it off.

He looked to Amp. "Give 'em hell. I have to go do some work of my own." He stood and then led the sexy lady away to an enclosed VIP booth.

Amp exhaled to try to release some tension, and then headed to Madam's office. Madam was sitting at her desk going through some paperwork. She looked a little overwhelmed and confused—the same emotions Amp was entertaining himself.

"Excuse me, Madam," Amp said, her eyes still glued to the papers before her. "I, uh, was told that you were the person to see about getting an outfit, so I can do amateur night tonight."

Madam looked up from her paperwork with a smile. She couldn't contain her excitement. It was as if she'd been waiting a lifetime to hear those very words coming from Amp's mouth. "I am," she confirmed, pushing aside the papers and standing up. Walking over to a metal cabinet, she pulled out a medium-sized box.

"Something in here should work just fine for you," she said as she set the box on her desk and started pulling out different thongs, G-strings, and various props.

Amp remained quiet as she laid the thong with an elephant trunk on the desk, but his facial expression told it all. He wasn't going to be caught dead, alive, or half naked in that thing. Following that, Madam set out a sailor hat and matching thong, a Tarzan loincloth, and several other equally wild outfits.

Amp took an apprehensive step closer to the collection spread out before him. Noticing the uncertain look on Amp's face, Madam said, "It's gonna be all right. G'on and shake what your momma gave you."

With an outfit in hand, Amp left for the dressing room. He may have exited Madam's office looking unsure, but he turned back to catch Madam wearing the look of a proud mother.

Chapter 13

Madam went back to her paperwork, but not even ten seconds later there was a light tap at her door. "Now what, Amp?" Madam said without even looking up from her desk as the door cracked open. Poor thing hadn't made it halfway to the locker room before his nerves got the best of him.

"I see you're still working hard."

That voice coming from her doorway gave Madam pause. Her eyes froze on the paper in front of her, and the pen fell out of her still fingers onto the desk. It sounded like . . . but was it? Sure it was. She'd know that voice anywhere, and it wasn't Amp's.

"Marcus," Madam's mouth spoke before her eyes looked up. She slowly raised her head to confirm the man's identity. Standing in the doorway was the same six foot one inch, nicely built man that had once captured her heart. He still looked the same, only now his head was bald. Where he once had just a beard, he now sported a salt-and-pepper goatee that was very attractive on him. "You look different. But still good." The words just fell out of Madam's mouth. She'd always been one to say whatever was on her mind anyway, so that was no surprise. "The hair, or should I say lack thereof—it works for you." She nodded her approval of the change in appearance.

Marcus ran his hand down his bald head and smiled. "I appreciate that. Coming from you, it must be true," he said. "Well, you, Miss Fox, look exactly the same." He tilted his head to the side and observed Madam.

"I hope I can take that as a compliment," Madam said.

"Of course. You look amazing." He stared at her with an appreciative smile on his face.

For Madam, it was as if he were looking right through her. She shifted in her chair a little bit. He wasn't making her feel uncomfortable; she was starting to feel like a high school girl alone in the hallway with her crush.

"Long time no see." She picked up the conversation in order to escape the awkward silence.

"Too long." His words were short, but his gaze into her eyes was long. He was looking for something, perhaps that spark that she once had for him.

Madam shifted in her chair again, almost as if she was trying to shift out of his viewpoint. His stare was penetrating. Her heart started beating a little faster with each breath. He was just as fine and sexy as she remembered. Not to mention that voice, that same deep baritone voice in which his words lingered like they had a natural echo.

Madam cleared her throat. He won the staring game, because in all her blushing, her eyes looked downward. This was the only man who could make Madam feel this way. There was nothing she could do to contain the butterflies in her stomach.

Marcus took a couple steps toward Madam's desk. "May I?" He extended his hand toward the chair.

"Oh, of course."

Staring at her the entire time, Marcus sat down. He followed her eyes down to the paperwork on her desk. After all, that's where hers kept darting off to. "If you're too busy . . ."

"Oh, no. I'm fine," Madam was quick to answer. She looked up and smiled. A part of her did not want that man to move a muscle.

"I agree. You are definitely fine."

Even his corny compliments had Madam's panties damp. Unlike some of the patrons who came to watch the men dance, Madam didn't have an extra pair of panties in her purse, so he needed to stop with all the Billy Dee Williams stuff. Truthfully, though, he didn't need to impersonate any man. This was just how Marcus was, how he'd always been: super fine, super slick, with a smooth, debonair aura about him.

"Thank you." Madam clasped her hands together. "So what brings you by Club Eden?"

"You." Straight to the point.

"What about me?"

"The last time we were, you know, connected, you were quite the busy bee managing that club. Didn't really have enough time for 'us,' to see where we could have taken things." He looked around. "But now I see you own your own club . . . which probably means you're just that much busier. That is, unless you've learned that life isn't always about work. You should work hard so you can play hard too." He leaned in. "So are you?"

Madam swallowed. "Am I what?"

"Ready to play . . . hard?"

Madam was caught up in watching his mouth as he pronounced the words. That mouth used to kiss her just right and in all the right places. She could have lived off those kisses forever, but she was a woman in a man's world trying to keep up and make things happen. Kisses and a relationship just weren't a priority in her life at the time. Marcus had always wanted them to be a priority, and she just couldn't give him that—not then, and certainly not now. Although she was good with what they had, Marcus wasn't a playboy with a different woman every day of the week. He wanted one woman and one woman only, and wanted to build something lasting. That woman had been Madam. When she couldn't give him the same in return, she wasn't even mad at him for calling it quits.

"Marcus, can I be honest with you?" Madam said.

He laughed. "Since when does Mary Fox ask permission to be honest?"

She smiled and looked downward.

"Shoot. What is it?" He encouraged her to proceed.

Madam looked back up at him. "When we were together, you were a good man. I can't say anything bad about you. And I'm sure you're an even better man, but nothing's changed with me, Marcus. Like you said . . . ." Madam raised her hands, gesturing to the office surroundings. "I'm not just managing a club, but I own one now. Which means—"

"That all work and no play still makes for a very dull girl. I get it." Marcus nodded with a sigh and then stood. "You know me, straight to the point. Never was one to play games or waste time. And so that I don't waste any more of yours or mine, I guess I'll be going. But hey, you can't blame a brotha for trying, can you?" He chuckled. "Guess when I'm in the neighborhood another three years from now, I'll check back in with you." He winked, trying to keep his head up after being shot down by the woman he'd once wanted to marry.

"I'm sorry, Marcus." Three years later it still hurt just as much to watch Marcus walk away.

"No need to apologize. Just figured a few years had gone by, I'd stop by and try my luck." He shrugged. "It was good seeing you again." He held out the palm of his hand.

Madam placed her hand inside of his. He lifted it to his mouth and placed a kiss on the back of her hand, staring directly into her eyes.

As he walked to the door, he stopped and made one last attempt to change her mind. "What about we just have lunch to see if, you know, we can at least try to pick up where things . . ." His words trailed off as Madam began shaking her head in the negative.

Although a part of Madam wanted to skip a lunch with him completely and go right back to his place and hit the sheets for old times' sake, she wasn't about to play with his mind like that. He deserved more, and right now, with all she had to deal with when it came to the club, she just couldn't give him more.

"A gentleman knows how to bow out gracefully." With that, Marcus left, closing the door behind him.

Madam went limp in her chair, exhaling so hard she almost blew the papers off her desk. "Lord have mercy." She began to fan herself as the lingering scent of Marcus's cologne brought back a wave of erotic memories.

Madam closed her eyes and went back to that time and place where not just his cologne, but everything about Marcus had intoxicated her. Madam hadn't always been all work. She knew how to play . . . at work. As a matter of fact, she could recall doing a little playing in her office at the old club when he'd dropped in on her one day. . . .

"Not right here," Madam had said to Marcus after he walked around her desk and began planting kisses all over her neck. He'd always

been spontaneous and romantic. Madam knew she could really stand to learn a thing or two from him about relaxing and letting go.

"Where at then? You don't seem like the type of lady who will let me take her out to my truck in the parking lot."

"Please. Now, you know we done did some thangs in that truck," Madam reminded him.

Marcus pulled away and looked at her as he tried to recall.

Madam decided to jog his memory. "When we were driving back from San Diego that night and you needed something to keep you awake." Madam raised an eyebrow.

A huge smile swept across his face. "Oh yeah, I remember now. Damn, that turns me on." He wrapped his arms around Madam's waist and went back to kissing her neck. "You ain't gon' leave me like this, are you?" He motioned down to the bulge in his pants.

"Marcus . . ." She tried to decline his sexual advances. Her mind was telling her no, that anyone could walk into that office at any minute and catch them. Even though a whole lot of what was about to go down in her office probably went down in the club champagne room daily, she was a professional. Her role wasn't to entertain on the job. Even with all that being

said, Madam's body was telling her yes as she began unbuttoning his shirt. She seemed to get wetter with each button she undid.

Before she knew it, she was returning tender kisses to Marcus's neck.

"Now that's what I'm talking about," Marcus said as he lifted his T-shirt over his head.

Madam moaned with pleasure as his hands caressed her breasts through her blouse. He slid his hands down to Madam's butt and cupped her sweet chocolate ass. He had big hands, so it fit perfectly inside them.

She could feel his hardness throbbing against her. Marcus's hands crawled down her skirt and then lifted it, revealing the sexy garter she was wearing.

"Wait, wait, wait." Madam placed her hand against Marcus's chest to push him away. They were both breathing heavily. "Did you lock the door when you came in?"

"Woman, who cares? We all grown folks up in here. Twenty-one and older. Ain't nobody gonna walk up in here and see nothing they ain't already seen—or done—before."

Madam looked at her sexy man, thought about it for a moment, and then looked at the door. With no further words, she pulled his head to her and stuck her tongue down his throat.

Marcus lifted her onto the desk and undid his pants while they kissed passionately. The sound of his zipper was a prelude for what was about to go down. With Madam already moist from pure passion, Marcus slid right into all her wetness, unable to muffle a moan as he entered her.

"Damn, you are wet," he whispered in her ear as he thrust himself in and out. She was literally dripping, and he loved that shit!

This wasn't the time to be all gentle and play with it. Their adrenaline was pumping, knowing that they could be exposed. It wasn't even necessarily that someone would see them— the idea of exhibitionism was actually pretty arousing—it was more the thought that they might have to stop what they were doing if they had company.

The faster Marcus went in and out of her, the louder the slapping sounds became, and the closer they were to climax.

Madam ran her nails down his back as he hit all the right spots. "Right there," she told him as her legs started to shake. That motherfucker could always find that spot.

"Is that your spot, baby?" It was rhetorical. He knew it was. He knew her inside and out.

Madam was so close to bursting that she couldn't even reply, but Marcus knew by the way she tightened herself around him that he was hitting it good.

"You 'bout to make me cum," he told her, going in even deeper. "Oh, shit, I'm 'bout to—"

Madam threw her hips right back at him, and he stopped holding back. He kissed her deeply as both reached the ultimate climax. . . .

Madam twitched in her chair at the thought of it now, sitting at her desk with a mound of paperwork before her. She didn't even smoke, but she felt like she needed a cigarette.

She looked up at the door through which Marcus had just exited. Maybe he was right, Madam thought. She'd been working hard all her life. Maybe, just maybe, it was time to play a little. After all, she hadn't played in quite a long time.

Looking down again at the mound of work before her, Madam sighed and asked herself, "Who am I kidding?" With the way things were looking, it definitely was not playtime.

Chapter 14

A short while later, Amp stood nervously backstage, waiting for his cue to go on.

"Ladies, ladies, ladies," DJ Dime spoke into the darkened room. "It is my pleasure to introduce to you this strong and sexy piece of a man. I know it's amateur night, but let me warn you, ladies. Something tells me that he is no amateur. He looks like he knows exactly what he's doing. Ladies, give it up for Amp!"

The women in the club began to whistle and cheer as the curtains slowly parted, giving them a full view of Amp's silhouette. Barefoot, wearing a wife beater and some khakis, Amp walked to the center of the stage. With every step, the women howled. Although Amp had chosen not to wear the entire uniform at the last minute, no one seemed to mind, including Madam, who had just entered the room to take a peek at her latest moneymaker.

The lights were low and the crowd was excited, tantalized by the shadow and shape of Amp's amazing physique, no longer hidden underneath that security shirt and jeans. Amp stood perfectly still as the music came on, even though everything in him wanted to shake the nerves away. He still couldn't believe what was about to go down. He was about to take it off for money. Willing himself to keep his mind on his ultimate goal, he prepared to grind for this crowd of horny, rowdy women.

The bass was deep and thick. The song Amp had chosen for his opening routine was called "Insomnia." It had a slow groove, and the lyrics were very provocative. He'd predicted that this would make the women hot and ready for his performance. It worked. They were on fire. As soon as he made his first move, someone screamed "Take it off!" But he was a teaser. He wanted to build them into a climax at the end, so he had to make them wait.

Amp moved just a little with every beat of the music, rolling his groin area slowly and intensely, making sure everybody watching knew that he had skills. DJ Dime put a spotlight on Amp's manhood. This drove the women in the audience crazy with anticipation.

Amp was a hit from the start. The audience absolutely loved the newest addition to the club. Amp, on the other hand, couldn't wait for his ten minutes of fame to come to an end—at least until the chants of the crowd helped him loosen up a bit. Then their excitement encouraged Amp to give them what they'd come for. It was too late to turn back now.

The cheering crowd lured Amp from one side of the stage to the other during the first song as he rolled his hips, moved his body seductively, and made eye contact with as many of the women as he could. Remembering what Babyface had told him, Amp looked at each woman as if she were his and he was dancing just for her.

Any time his thoughts wandered back to the reality of what he was doing, Amp forced himself to let it go. He couldn't get caught up in his thoughts; he needed this money if he was ever going to move on with his life. He decided to get out of the way and let his body, the music, and the crowd take over. He became animalistic, using the audience's energy and lust to bring out the freak in him.

Eventually, Amp wasn't even moving his body to the beat of the music anymore, but to the tune of the crowd. As the women got louder and louder, his movements got stronger and stronger. The women were making music of their own, so to speak, and Amp was dancing to it.

By song number two, Amp was in his zone. He had chosen a gritty, Dirty South strip-club song that had the crowd on their feet, dancing and clapping too. The beat had that Atlanta bounce to it, with a heavy bass, and every time the drums hit, he thrust his manhood as hard as he could at some lucky woman in the crowd, paying special attention to the big girls.

It had turned into a wild party. Amp started removing some of his clothes, starting with his wife beater. The ladies lost their minds when Amp exposed his six pack. His upper body looked like something most of the women had only dreamed about—literally.

"Jesus!" a woman called out, and it wasn't because of the one foot cross tattooed on the left side of Amp's chest.

Amp stood there momentarily and let the women take in the view. All the while, he gazed across the room at the ladies, running his hand over his five o'clock shadow. Amp did this intentionally, to make the women contemplate which one of them he was going to take home that night. He was being slick and strategic in making sure he turned them on. This may have been only his second time on that stage, but he did know women and what they liked. Amp was surprised to find that this whole stripping routine came very easy to him. Maybe he was a natural, he thought with amusement.

Amp removed his pants one leg at a time, letting the women take in the full sight of him and his bulge. He smiled, confident in how well-endowed he was. Then he turned to the back of the stage and shook his ass, knowing that probably every woman in the room was imagining what it would be like to grab that ass while he was deep inside of them. He then turned back around to let them see his quadriceps of steel. One woman reached her hand out and stroked the air as if she were running her hands up and down the maze of definition on his torso.

By the handful, ones, fives, tens, and twenties floated to the floor next to Amp's feet. He could see that he was making more on this stage in ten minutes than he had made all week at Mr. Lam's store. The lure of fast money was definitely pulling him in.

DJ Dime's voice floated above the crowd. "We have a bachelorette in here tonight. Nina, where you at? Raise your hand."

At a table in the middle of the crowd, a group of women started whooping and hollering, pointing at a petite woman wearing a tiara with a veil attached. Her thin-framed glasses and the way she tentatively raised her hand made her look like an innocent little secretary whose friends had twisted her arm to get her to the club.

DJ Dime threw a spotlight on the table. "Since this is her last week of freedom," she said, "Amp, would you be so kind as to bring her up on stage and give her a treat? Let's send her off into marital bliss with a bang! But go easy on her. We wouldn't want her leaving her man at the altar."

Amp obliged without hesitation. Babyface had told him that audience participation was a sure way to increase your night's earnings, and he was becoming pretty relaxed anyway, now that the money was flowing freely onto the stage.

Apparently the woman's friends loved the idea of the bride-to-be getting some special attention. As Amp approached and she shrank back in her chair, they began nudging her, urging her to go to the stage. She finally relented and stood up, taking Amp's hand, which he'd been holding out for her. He grabbed her chair with his free hand and carried that up to the stage with them. It was time to see if that YouTube video would pay off.

The bride, who whispered shyly that her name was Nina, pretended she wanted to go back and sit with her girls, blushing and shaking her head; but it was all for show, because she was not fighting Amp one bit.

As they made it to the stage, the third song started to play. This time it was "Adore," a Prince song, and the women went wild. Amp placed the chair in the middle of the stage and sat Nina in it. He circled around her. She was his sensual prey.

"I ain't never wanted to be another broad in my life, but I damn sure wish I was her right about now," one of the women in the front row yelled out.

Between Babyface's instructions, the videos Amp had watched on YouTube, and a couple of freaky nights he'd had with ex-lovers, Amp gave Nina the private dance of her life—only it wasn't so private, as all eyes watched Amp's every move. He had Nina sweating and cooing without even touching her. He came close enough to her, though, so that she could smell his scent, hear his breath, and feel the heat of his incredible body. He made her—and the horny onlookers—salivate with desire.

Feeling inspired to go all in as heaps of paper money cascaded to the stage, Amp spread her legs apart into a split. He stood slowly and picked her up effortlessly. Her waist was level with his head, so that to the audience, it looked as if Nina were being kissed in the most intimate of places. The way she was suspended in the air looked like some sort of erotic Cirque du Soleil.

His glutes tightened, and his razor sharp calf muscles went to work in balancing the woman. She was no longer acting like she didn't want to participate. This future bride had given in to the ride of a lifetime, and her friends were astonished. Everyone in that room had just witnessed her climax. Amp had achieved his goal.

Those women lost it. So much money went flying Amp's way that if there were any other dancers left to hit the stage, all the women had left in their purses to give were bobby pins, gum wrappers, and lip-gloss.

Amp placed the blushing bride-to-be back down on the chair as the song ended. His body, now glistening with sweat, was a sight indeed.

The lights went dark, and Amp left the stage the same way he had come—with the crowd on their feet, wanting more from him. Now he only hoped it was all worth it. He'd find out just as soon as he counted his earnings.

Madam stood in her office doorway, nodding her head in approval. Amp acknowledged her, as well as the crowd that was yelling for an encore. They were demanding more; now Amp would be left with the decision of whether he would give them what they desired.

Chapter 15

After his performance, it was back to work as usual for Amp, although he definitely had to come down off of a high. He hadn't had attention from a woman in years, so now to be dealing with a room full of women showing him that much love was somewhat overwhelming.

He returned to his position as club security and continued his regular duties for the night, every now and then having to bring his thoughts back to reality after traveling to his moments on the stage. Club Eden had certainly reminded him just how beautiful the female species was and how it felt to be next to a woman.

Around two in the morning, women began to leave the club.

"Be safe," Amp told a group of them as they passed by.

"You t—" One woman started to return the same sentiment, until she looked up at Amp. Squinting in the semi-darkness, she said, "Wait a minute. Aren't you that guy that was just inside dancing?"

Amp had already recognized her as one of the big tippers who'd been seated in the front row. Apparently she'd been staring too hard at his body to get a good look at his face, because now that he was in his security uniform, she wasn't sure it was Amp who had been dancing.

He decided to play incognito. She'd been pretty rowdy in the club, and now that it was nearly closing time, he didn't want her getting worked up again. In addition, he was feeling slightly embarrassed to be recognized as a guy who'd just taken off his clothes for money. These women didn't know his story. As far as they were concerned, he was just some gigolo, and Amp didn't like the way that felt.

"That's too bad. We were gonna come back next week and spend some more money on him," she said.

She and her girls were all friendly smiles as they said good night and walked away. Nothing in the way they looked at him made Amp feel like they were judging him. Perhaps he was over-thinking it and didn't need to feel embarrassed. Perhaps what he needed to feel was happy that he was a hit, and that they were willing to come back with more money next week.

With that thought in mind, Amp called out, "I think that guy you're talking about might be back next week."

The big tipper from the front row turned around and said, "We'll see," tapping her purse.

"See you then," Amp said under his breath as he headed inside the club.

Amp made his way toward the stage area. He spotted Madam over at the DJ booth talking to Dime. Walking toward them, he pulled the tips that he'd made that night out of his pocket.

"Excuse me, Madam," Amp respectfully interrupted. "What's the usual percentage that I'm supposed to give you and the DJ?"

Madam held her finger up to pause her conversation with Dime, then she turned to Amp. "On amateur night you can keep it all. If you come on as a regular dancer, I get fifteen percent and the DJ gets five. So tonight, it looks like I'm the one who owes you." Madam pulled out some bills. "Here's your doorman pay for the night, minus the time that you were in here turning my place out."

Amp lowered his head in embarrassment, although he couldn't help but smile at her compliment.

"You really should consider doing this again," Madam suggested. "You're very handsome, have an amazing body, and the women are going nuts over you."

She must have sensed some hesitation in Amp's body language, because when she saw

that the compliments weren't enough to convince him, she tried another tactic, appealing
to his work ethic. "You know, when I first met
you, you seemed to be very focused, like you're
determined to make something of yourself. You
could make a lot of money on that stage in a
short amount of time—for whatever it is you're
working so hard for. Trust me, I know a good fit
when I see it, and you are good for business."

"Thank you. I'll think about it. But tomorrow,
I'll be back on the door."

Amp really did want to have some time to
think about it, so he switched the subject in a
hurry. Dime was still standing there, watching
them have a conversation, so he decided to
introduce himself to her. They hadn't formally
met yet, because she was already in the booth
working by the time Amp showed up each night.

"I'm Amp," he said, suddenly realizing how
attractive she was. Up until now, Dime had
basically been a figure in a booth, a voice over
the mic. Now he was seeing her figure up close
and personal.

She stood about six feet tall in heels, which
meant she was at least five foot seven without
them. The way the club lights were hitting her
pretty brown skin, it only complemented
her glow. She didn't wear a whole lot of makeup,
but she definitely didn't need to. She had natural

beauty that didn't need to be covered by heavy cosmetics. Her long, thick lashes flickered above her big, brown eyes, and full lips that spread into a smile, revealing pretty white teeth.

Amp wasn't good with guessing women's sizes, but she had a nice and natural shape. She was fit and still curvy. She wasn't dressed like one would imagine a typical DJ to dress either. Those jeans she was wearing, that tank top, and those pink-and-white manicured nails made her hotter than any DJ Amp had ever seen.

"Allison." Dime smiled, and small dimples dented her russet bronze cheeks. "But my working name is DJ Dime." She stared Amp right in the eyes. She'd already stared at his body for ten minutes while he did his show, so she knew what he was working with.

"Good to meet you." Amp nodded. There was a long moment where neither of them wanted to break eye contact. Finally Amp spoke up, not wanting to seem too forward, no matter how much he was feeling a spark between them. "Well, I guess I'll see you ladies tomorrow," he said, tucking his money back in his pocket.

"Definitely," Dime said with a half-smile. She and Madam enjoyed the view as he walked away.

***

Amp had just gotten his workout on at the park and was jogging up the street to the house when he saw Mr. Barrett standing on the porch with a briefcase in hand. He assumed that his parole officer was waiting on him.

"How's it going, Mr. Barrett?" Amp said as he walked up the porch steps.

"Fine. How are you?"

Amp sensed that Mr. Barrett couldn't care less how he was doing, asking only out of formality. Still, he replied, "I'm gettin' by."

"I heard about the robbery."

"Yeah. It cost me my job." Amp shrugged. No need to go into details as if Mr. Barrett cared. "It is what it is."

"You didn't know the guy or have anything to do with it?"

Amp was slightly taken aback, but he didn't let it show. He had to remember that to his parole officer, he was just another ex-con, and if he lost his cool, he would be back in jail before he even made it out of the halfway house. Amp gave the parole officer the benefit of the doubt, telling himself that Mr. Barrett was just trying to stay on top of his job—and his clients. So, Amp simply replied, "No, and no."

"Okay, I had to ask. Just like I have to ask you to drop today."

"Okay. You got the cup?" Amp said it matter-of-factly, to let Mr. Barrett know that he had nothing to hide.

Mr. Barrett pulled a container out of his brief-case and handed it to Amp. "Do I need to watch you?" Mr. Barrett asked.

"Nah, I'm clean."

"Go ahead. You got ninety seconds." Mr. Barrett raised his wrist, displaying his watch. He really was putting Amp on a countdown.

Amp darted into the house. A minute later, he returned the cup with his sample back to Mr. Barrett. Mr. Barrett took it, nodding just once before he walked off the porch and back to his car.

Paul joined Amp on the steps, and the two men watched Mr. Barrett back out of the drive-way, shoot Amp an unsettling look, then drive away.

"Is he always like this?" Amp asked Paul.

"Pretty much." Paul thought for a moment and then turned to Amp. "I'm going to test you today too."

"For what?" Clearly Paul knew he had just given a sample to Mr. Barrett. Why did he want one as well?

Watching Mr. Barrett's brake lights as his car turned at the corner, Paul said, "Just to be on the safe side." He headed back in the house, and Amp followed behind him.

"Okay," Amp said. What else could he say? Like Paul always stressed, he was the one who ran that house. Amp wasn't about to put up a fight, especially since he was clean. He concluded that working at a bar would give people doubt, but he knew the test would come back clear.

"So how was your first time?" Madam asked Amp, who was posted up at the front entrance of the club. He and Babyface had been standing there talking and laughing for a few minutes when Madam came out of the club and joined the conversation.

"It was okay," Amp replied. He wasn't about to tell her the whole truth, how his nerves had him five seconds from running off that stage before the hook of the first song had a chance to play. "The money was good." Now that was the truth. "Made like three hundred fifty dollars in only three songs."

Babyface dapped Amp and then headed back inside the club, leaving Amp to talk with Madam.

Madam nodded. "That's good money to make in that short amount of time. Is it something you'd do again?"

"I don't know. Maybe." Amp had been asking himself the same question ever since he left the stage. His answer constantly changed as he continued to toy with the idea. The money was good, but was that really what he wanted as a career move? Then again, was being a security guard at a strip club any more prestigious? The reality was Amp was an ex-con, so at this point, anything legal was a step up.

"Good," Madam said. "Because I had a client request you for a private party. You could make three times as much as you made the other night."

The look of uncertainty did not leave Amp's face, even at the prospect of a bigger payday. "Madam, with all due respect, I'm going to have to pass. I don't think the house supervisor is gonna go for that private party stuff." Paul had been good about Amp working at the corner store and even up in the club. He hadn't really pressed him too hard, if at all. Amp figured he'd better leave well enough alone.

"Would he allow you to dance here regularly?"

"Possibly. I can ask."

"You should. The ladies were loving you, so you'll definitely make some good money. Think about it. But if you're going to do it on a more regular basis, you'll eventually have to get a little more creative with your routine. The women love new blood—or should I say fresh meat?—but eventually they'll want you to mix it up some. Maybe incorporate some of that stuff I saw you doing on the bars at the park."

"Okay. I'll let you know," he said, and she nodded then turned to go back into the building.

"Madam," Amp called to her.

She stopped, holding back her smirk. She knew exactly what was coming next.

"If Mr. Harold approves it, when can I start?"

"Next week. You can do amateur night again. It'll give you a little time to work on your routine. Then, you can start full-time Thursday if you want."

"When I'm not on stage, can I still work the door?" Amp didn't want any down time. He wanted to stay on the clock and keep making money.

"No," she said. Amp was momentarily disappointed, until she explained, "You'll be making money in between your sets. Those women are going to keep you busy, trust me. I can't have my new star out here working the front door. It's not sexy."

"Okay." It sounded good to Amp. As long as he was making money, it was all making sense.

Chapter 16

Amp was knocking out his morning chores, which today included trash duty, dusting, and vacuuming. The majority of the house was hardwood floors, so the task of running the vacuum was confined to the living room only. If the housemates wanted their bedrooms swept, that was their personal responsibility, which prevented another housemate from having an excuse to be in their room. It was pretty early, so if any of his housemates hadn't yet awakened, they were surely about to, as Amp plugged in the sweeper and went to work.

The living room wasn't that big, so it wouldn't take but five minutes to hit the entire room. When Amp did things, he liked to do them right the first time. Unlike most of the other housemates, who barely made an effort to clean, he moved the furniture around and cleaned the hidden areas.

He had just put the couch back in place and was wrapping up the vacuum cord when he noticed flashing lights out of the corner of his eye. Almost instantaneously he heard someone banging on the door.

Amp set aside the vacuum and went to answer the door. Standing on the other side of the screen were Mr. Barrett and the same officers who'd taken Melvin away.

"I need you to step away from the door, Mr. Anthony," Mr. Barrett barked before Amp could even fix his mouth to greet them.

Amp backed up quickly, with a blanket of confusion on his face. The next thing he knew, the officers were storming into the house. They headed straight toward Amp, one taking out his handcuffs.

"What's going on here?" Paul asked, rushing into the living room.

Mr. Barrett, straightening his pants at the waist with his thumbs, was glad to tell him. "Well, the drug test for Mr. Anthony here shows alcohol in his system, which is a direct violation of his parole."

"That's bullshit!" Amp interjected. "I haven't had a drink in years."

"The test doesn't lie," Mr. Barrett said arrogantly. He had a straight face, but his eyes were smiling. Amp sensed that this guy was enjoying the moment.

One officer held Amp, while the other hand-cuffed him. Amp didn't put up a fight, although the bulging veins on the sides of his forehead clearly displayed his desire to take some heads off.

"Amp, be cool." Paul gestured with a flat hand for Amp to bring his temper down a notch. "I'll handle this." He turned to Mr. Barrett. "Let me talk to you real quick. It'll only take a second." Without even waiting for Mr. Barrett's consent, Paul walked a few steps away from where the two officers had Amp hemmed up.

Mr. Barrett followed, shooting Amp a dirty look as he passed by. Amp didn't back down, staring right in his eyes. He knew he had done nothing wrong. The problem was, he also knew the reputation the LAPD had when it came to their treatment of young black men, so Amp was nervous. He said a quick prayer, asking God not to let him go back to jail, and not to let all the progress he'd made be in vain. He hadn't prayed in a long time, but he hoped that God still recognized his voice.

Opening his eyes after the prayer, Amp looked toward Mr. Barrett and Paul, who both had scowls on their faces. In the small living room, he was able to hear their conversation, and he couldn't believe what was being said.

"Paul, I really don't have time for this," Barrett started. "I know you take a liking to these boys, but they ain't nothing but animals and street thugs that need to stay locked up."

Paul got straight to his point, ignoring Mr. Barrett's prejudiced assessment of the men in the house. "I tested Amp five minutes after you left," Paul informed him. "I ran it through the county screening center and it came back clean."

A crimson flush took over Mr. Barrett's usually pale complexion. "Well, they must have made a mistake," he said, sounding flustered.

Across the room, Amp's heart started pounding. Maybe God had heard his voice after all.

"No. You made a mistake—or at least you're about to make the biggest one of your life," Paul warned him. "Tampering with federal drug tests . . . Forget about losing your job, benefits, and pension. Do you know how much time in jail you could get for that?" Paul returned the same dirty look to Mr. Barrett that Mr. Barrett had given Amp.

Mr. Barrett was silent, but his facial expression said it all: *Oh, shit!*

Paul leaned in a little closer to Mr. Barrett, but Amp could still hear his matter-of-fact tone as he said, "From here on out, I will test these guys in this house, and you will happily sign off on my results. Otherwise, I will turn my test and yours over to the D.A. and let them toss you in there with some of the same 'animals' you had locked up. You got me?"

"Yes," Mr. Barrett replied at a level that was almost inaudible.

"Good. Now feel free to get your goofy ass out of here." Paul motioned to the door.

Practically tripping over his feet in embarrassment, Mr. Barrett turned around. He said to the officers, "There's been some kind of mix-up. This young man is clean. Let's go." Without even waiting for the officers to free Amp, Mr. Barrett exited the house.

Amp knew that if he was able to hear the conversation, then the officers had heard it too, but they didn't react. They simply un-cuffed Amp and followed Mr. Barrett out the door, giving no apologies. Amp wondered if they had been in on the scam all along.

Rubbing his wrists in the spot where the cuffs had been squeezing them, Amp said to Paul, "Wow, he tried to set me up?"

This explained why Paul had insisted that Amp do the second urine sample after Mr. Barrett already took one. Paul must have had his suspicions about the parole officer. The whole situation was shocking. Amp had always suspected that Mr. Barrett didn't like the men who kept him employed, but he never would have imagined that Barrett would jeopardize his job by setting up false test results.

Unfortunately, Amp was no stranger to that level of hatred and prejudice. He knew all too well that whether imprisoned or free, men of color could never truly escape the ugly effects of racism in America.

Glaring out the door as he watched the police car leaving, Paul replied, "I knew there was something off about him." He shook his head and pointed at Amp. "You just make sure you keep your nose clean. I'm putting my job on the line here. You make me out to be an idiot and I'm dragging you back to prison my damn self. Understood?"

Amp exhaled. "Loud and clear."

Paul walked into the kitchen, and Amp finished putting away the vacuum. The day had just begun, but he hoped like hell that this was the most dramatic thing that would happen all day.

Later on that night, it was closing time at Club Eden and the last few customers were filing out of the club. It was amateur night, and once again Amp had put on one hell of a show. Madam could call it amateur night all she wanted to, but there was nothing amateur about Amp's performance.

"You are a natural at this," Madam told Amp after his set. "You sure you haven't done this before?"

A few women in the audience had asked Amp the same question. The way Amp moved, he had to have been born with that talent. There was no way his performance was the result of a couple of YouTube videos and a crash course session with Babyface. But it was.

"So it's official. You're starting full-time to-morrow night, right?" Madam asked Amp as the two stood in her office.

Amp stuffed a knot of bills into his pocket. "Yes, ma'am." There were no ifs, ands, or buts, and absolutely no indecisiveness this time around. With the money Amp had made to-night, which was at least three hundred more than he'd made last week, his mind was made up. Good-bye, security, and hello, full-time dancer . . . and the hell with looking for a sec-ond job. This was plenty. Gone was the feeling of being embarrassed. Since when was making good money a cause for shame?

"Good," Madam said happily. "Let's handle this business."

"Now, you said for me to be a little creative with my routines. That's what I'm going to do. I'll probably come in early tomorrow and the rest of the week to work on stuff. Is that cool?" When Amp decided to do something, he went all in to make it happen. If he was going to be a stripper, then he was going to be the best stripper he could be. Amp wanted Madam to know that he was a man who took his job seriously, no matter what it was.

He was now fully committed, which put a smile on Madam's face. "Of course. Any time after two p.m. someone will be here."

"Cool. See you tomorrow." Amp turned to leave.

"I'm going your way if you want a ride."

"No, thanks. I don't mind. It's a short walk," Amp said over his shoulder.

"Okay. Good night."

Amp headed out of the club. As he crossed the parking lot, he saw Dime loading some of her equipment into her car.

"You need a hand?" Amp asked.

Dime looked up, struggling to put a mixer in her car. "I got it, thanks," she said, although the strain of lifting the equipment was evident in the way she was breathing.

Amp watched her for a few more seconds. He was reminded of how his mother used to struggle trying to carry in all the grocery bags after a week's worth of shopping. "You go on and finish playing with your friends," she told Amp one time when he'd tried to help her. He obliged her at first, until a dozen eggs ended up cracked on the walkway. He learned from that to go with his instincts and help her anyway.

Following those instincts, Amp walked over to help Dime. "Here, let me do that for you." He lifted the mixer out of her hands and noticed Dime checking him out as he bent over to place it in her car. As for him, he couldn't help but notice how amazing she smelled.

"I said I got it." Dime sounded slightly perturbed as she tried to pull it away from Amp even though he already had it halfway in the car.

"Look," he said, "you're a lady with a bunch of expensive equipment out here at two-thirty in the morning." Amp wanted her to understand that he was helping not to insult her, but to keep her safe. No woman needed to be caught off guard in the middle of the night with her hands full so she couldn't defend herself.

Clearly Dime hadn't thought about all that. She looked at her Numark Mixdeck Quad, laptop, headphones, and mics spread on the ground around her. All that expensive equipment might in fact make her a pretty tempting target. "When you put it that way . . ." she relented, letting him put away the mixer and all the other equipment too. Amp liked being her knight in shining armor.

"That should do it," he said as he repositioned the last piece of equipment.

"Thanks," she said, closing the trunk.

"No problem. Oh, before I forget—I'm going to write down a couple cues for the lights and the music for my set tomorrow night. I'll get them to you before we open."

"Okay, but . . ." She paused.

"What?"

"Well, you're gonna need a better name than Amp."

Amp raised his eyebrows, wondering if he should be offended.

"I'm just saying. I mean, Babyface, El Fuego, Dr. Feelgood, Casanova . . . Amp." It sounded so flat when she said it, so ordinary next to the others. "You need a stage name like everybody else, don't you think?"

"Good point," he said. "Any suggestions?"

"Well, not that I'm watching you," she said with a smirk, "but I see the way you put the women under some kind of spell. Like it's magic or something. So . . . maybe Black Magic."

Amp didn't look convinced at first, but after saying it a couple of times in his head, he had to admit it had a kind of ring to it. "Black Magic. I guess that's cool."

"Black Magic. That works." Of course Dime agreed, since she was the one who came up with it in the first place. "So you're really going to do this dancing thing full time, huh?"

"I'm trying to get this money." Amp was owning his career move. No excuses.

"That's too bad." She shook her head and looked down.

"Why?"

"'Cause I don't date dancers," she stated flatly, giving Amp a look like it was his loss and then walking over to the driver's side door.

"That's okay," Amp said quickly. "I don't date DJs."

They both shared a laugh that started off jovial but faded off into an awkward pause with each of them wondering how serious the other one was.

"Well, I'll see you tomorrow," Amp said, cutting through the silence.

Dime nodded her farewell and watched Amp walk away. Even though he never looked back to acknowledge it, he knew she was watching. He had to admit that it felt good knowing a woman was watching him . . . while he was still fully dressed.

He thought about her eyes the whole way home. She was gonna be trouble. Good trouble.

Chapter 17

The lights at Club Eden began to dim upon the patrons who were buzzing with anticipation for what was to come. They knew exactly what the lowering of the lights meant: It was show time, and things were about to get hot and crazy up in there.

Smoke began to fill the stage, and when there was smoke up in Club Eden, there was surely fire to follow. DJ Dime's sultry voice came through the speakers, letting them know that the moment they had been waiting for—all week, for some of them—was only seconds away.

"Ladies, hold on to your seats. It's about to get hot in here." Dime began to fan herself for effect, even though none of the women were watching her in the DJ booth. The same way the dancers took on a persona, she was fulfilling her role as well. "Welcome to the stage, Black Magic!"

The song "How Does It Feel?" by D'Angelo started as the curtain rose slowly, eventually revealing Amp's silhouette hanging upside down in the shadowy darkness. The back of his knees rested on the bar, and his arms were folded across his chest. That was enough to get a couple women on their feet, eager to see just what kind of tricks ol' Black Magic was about to perform.

Amp slowly lowered himself down, facing away from the crowd full of women who were hungry for whatever they were about to be fed. Judging from the level of excitement in the room, they were willing to try anything on the menu, because they knew that Club Eden only served Grade-A Choice, top of the line. With a routine actually lined up, instead of just freestyling like he'd done on amateur night, Amp had never felt more confident in what he was about to supply to his demanding patrons.

Even the darkness and the smoke couldn't hide Amp's cut shoulder blades and back muscles. All at once the song changed, the lights came up a little, and Amp turned to face the audience. The women went crazy.

There he stood, sheer perfection in their eyes, right down to his wicked smile accented by a strong, defined jaw. Amp figured it didn't take much for the ladies to fantasize about whether those jaw bones could do what every other bone in his body was doing to them: making them wet with wonder.

Only a beat here and there of the music could be heard. The artist's voice had been long drowned out by the women creating their own lyrics of chants and cheers. Not even if she wanted to could Dime be the voice of reason in this insane riot as underwear and money flew to the stage.

Amp made his way onto the floor and grabbed one of the lucky ladies to come and partake in his magic. He gradually led her to the stage, gyrating around her the whole time. He could feel all eyes on him, so he deliberately took his time. Then, in one quick action, he picked the lady up and laid her on the floor.

He got up and began to walk around her in a circle, teasing her and the crowd with the movements of his body. Standing right above her head, he started to roll his hips as he slowly lowered himself until he was in her face. She grabbed his ass with both hands, and he continued to pump in and out as if he were making love to her face. Then in one motion he flipped her over onto her stomach, crawling up her body while he kept rolling his hips in a circle.

He whispered in her ear, "Do you like it?" as his bulge lightly caressed her ass. She was literally screaming at this point. Drawers, money, and even credit cards showered Amp and the woman on stage. Amp couldn't help but wonder if the women really carried extra panties in their purses and threw them on the stage for show, or if that many women were really going home minus an undergarment.

For three songs straight, Amp gave them a performance they would never forget. He had taken Madam's advice and incorporated some of his workout moves on the bar and yoga positions on the floor, on the tables, and on the chairs. Amp then worked his way around the room, dancing, disrobing, and leaving the women spellbound.

Only those bold enough, or horny enough, took the liberty of copping a feel of Amp's manhood. Manicured nails slightly grazed his chest. Soft, feminine hands were squeezing his arms and smacking his ass. Women were doing everything but screaming out, "Pick me! Choose me!" in order to get a moment of special and exclusive attention from him.

At the end of the final song, his body was dripping with sweat and wet desire. Amp gathered his money and put it in a bag he had placed on the side of the stage before the show. He grabbed the outfit he had shed and headed for the locker room, feeling confident that he'd left all of the ladies feeling satisfied. The overstuffed bag made him sure he had made more money than both amateur nights put together.

He was anxious to go count it, but just before he made it to the locker room, Madam stopped him.

"Black Magic, huh?" she said, a smile flirting with the corners of her mouth. "I like it."

"Thanks." He appreciated Madam's approval, kind of the same way he appreciated Paul's no-nonsense but still respectful attitude. Without his own mother and father in his life, Amp felt this was the closest he was going to get to parental figures.

"I need you back on the floor quick. Got several ladies that want private dances."

Here she was talking about private dances again, Amp thought. They must have been real moneymakers. She had piqued his curiosity. "What exactly goes on in these private dances?"

"Just dancing," Madam informed him. She shrugged, as if to say, "What else do you think goes on?"

Amp gave Madam an unsure look. When the roles were reversed and the strippers were women, private dances usually meant a whole lot more than just a dance. Could it really be true that some women would pay for a private dance if there was no sex involved? It was hard to believe, but at the same time, Madam knew Amp's situation, and he didn't think she'd set him up for something that could send him back to jail. He decided to give her the benefit of the doubt.

"Okay," he said. "Just give me a few minutes and I'll be back out on the floor."

Before going on into the locker room, Amp headed over to the DJ booth.

"Was that what you wanted?" Dime asked Amp, removing her Beats by Dre headphones and resting them around her neck.

"Perfect, thank you."

Dime nodded her head to the beat of the song that was playing in between sets. "You looked good up there."

"I thought you weren't watching."

Dime didn't reply, just fiddled around with her equipment.

"Can you hold this for me 'til the end of the night?" Amp asked, extending the bag of cash he'd just collected in tips. He looked down at his body, covered in nothing but a G-string. "Clearly I don't have anywhere to put it."

Dime laughed as she took the money. "Oh, so you do have a sense of humor."

Amp turned away, mainly so that Dime wouldn't see him blush. His father had taught him that when you remain in serious mode, people take you seriously. This had been instilled in Amp at a young age, and he had always displayed such manners, especially in the workplace. In jail it had been a defense mechanism too. That was the last place he wanted people to think he was an easygoing, push-over kind of guy. He straightened up his face and turned back to Dime.

"You're always so serious," she said.

Amp couldn't argue with that fact.

Dime stuffed the money under the counter. "Well, you better get back to work, Black Magic." She winked.

"Thanks." Amp walked away, disappearing into the locker room . . . just like magic.

"Yo, Amp, man—twelve o'clock," Babyface said as Amp approached him near the bar.

Amp turned around and looked in the direction where Babyface was pointing. Straight ahead, close to the back, Amp saw a woman settled at a table alone. Her legs were crossed, and her chocolate thigh was peeking out of the red wrap dress she was wearing. The dress was cut low, and the cleavage was lovely. Her hair was slicked back in a bun. A small diamond-encrusted circle charm dangled from the thin platinum chain around her neck. As her crossed leg dangled, Amp noticed the same red bottom on her shoes that he'd seen on Madam's the day he first met her at the park.

Seeing that she now had Amp's attention from all the way across the room, the woman did a slight wave at Amp and then leaned over to her drink. She cupped her hands around the bowl of the glass like she was caressing balls, then wrapped her lips, which were covered in a plum sparkle lipstick, around her straw.

Her seductive movements had both Babyface and Amp in a trance. Babyface, with his eyes glued to the woman, said, "I swear if you don't go over there and holler at her, I'm going to."

Amp stared at her a little longer. Clearly she knew she was being watched as she put on a show, running her hand up her leg as if she had an itch she needed to scratch. The come hither look she was giving Amp made him want to be the one who scratched it.

"What's up with her?" Amp asked Babyface.

"She's one of Madam's friends. I hear she just got a divorce when she found out her husband was having multiple affairs with strippers."

"Damn," Amp said. "Dude must have been a fool messing around with a woman like that at home."

"Yeah," Babyface agreed. "And now she wants a private dance from you. Guess you're her revenge," he said with a laugh.

"Word," Amp said, almost mesmerized. He looked her over slowly and exhaled. It had been a long time since he had been with a woman in any capacity, especially in a one-on-one intimate setting, and this grown-ass woman right here was gonna be a problem—in the best possible way.

Amp wasn't even sure how to approach her; he just knew it had to be done.

"Well, I see one of my regulars," Babyface said to Amp, snapping him out of his trance. "I'm gonna go and let you handle that." He looked at the woman one last time. "If you can." He hit Amp on the back and then walked away.

Amp swallowed hard and rubbed his hands together. He wasn't quite sure what he should say to her. He practiced in his head: *Hey, lovely lady, I was told you wanted a lap dance.* No, that wouldn't work. That sounded corny, the whole "lovely lady" bit.

YouTube might have taught him how to move his ass, but the lesson he hadn't been schooled in was the shit-talking game that went on in all strip clubs. He would definitely have to ask his fellow dancers about that aspect of the business, but right now he was a day late and a dollar short—that would be literally, if he didn't hurry up and make his way over to ol' girl.

Clearing his throat and taking a deep breath, Amp headed over toward the woman. On his way over, he mumbled a couple more things he could possibly say, but everything sounded so rehearsed, rightfully so, since that's exactly what he was doing. By the time he made it over to her table, all his concerns about what to say were for naught, since she spoke first.

"So you gonna dance for Mommy?" she said, smacking her hand on the hundred dollar bill she had laid on the table. From across the room she might have seemed as harmless as a kitten, but the lioness had definitely come out of her, and she was ready to get right down to business.

"Right here?" Amp asked.

"I can think of some other places, but for now, right here will be fine." She leaned back in her chair and got her *Basic Instinct* on, spreading her legs just wide enough to let Amp know she would not be throwing any panties at him tonight, because she wasn't wearing any. Amp appreciated the sight of her fresh Brazilian for a moment. Other than in the pages of the magazines that had helped him get through his time in prison, he hadn't seen anything like this in five years.

He realized he didn't have to waste his time coming up with something to say. Words were not what she was the least bit interested in. It was all about action, so Amp didn't hesitate to give her just what she wanted.

Amp's nerves were settled as the woman's erotic aura set the atmosphere for him to go all in with the private dance. He started with the grinding of his hips. She rocked her head back and forth to the beat of his hips. He turned around, putting his hands behind his head while he continued to grind. He placed his hand around her throat, gently easing her back in her seat. Then he slid both hands from her neck to her shoulders and down her arms, all while still rolling his hips. He could feel her goose-bumps as he continued moving his strong, manly hands lower to her waist, then to her hips, and further south to her knees.

Amp reached up and spread her legs open without breaking eye contact. He could tell this turned the woman on immensely as her breathing became more rapid. He leaned in slowly, stopping inches away from her pretty little shaved honeypot. Amp took in a breath and softly blew it on her now dripping wet lips. She jerked just a little as that tingle sprinted up her spine. Within seconds, the woman in red was gripping his ass cheeks the same way she had been gripping her glass just moments ago.

Although no words were being spoken, a lot was being said. Amp placed a hand on each of her knees while returning a seductive stare into her eyes. Never once did she look away and play shy girl like some of the other women would do. She let Amp know that she wasn't the least bit intimidated by his flawless physique, chiseled face, strong muscles, and tough attitude.

Tonight, the woman in red was putting her husband's alimony to good use as she slapped another hundred dollar bill down on the table. Amp danced like there was no tomorrow. He made her feel special and wanted again. Before the night was over, perhaps she'd be calling up her ex and telling him that she got it—that she now understood how one could fall in love with a stripper.

There was someone else in the room who understood how one could possibly fall for a stripper, but Amp was too caught up in the dance and the fact that the woman in red had laid yet a third hundred dollar bill on the table to notice Dime watching him. When he did look up and see her staring, he decided to give her a show. He wanted Dime to know, just in case things ever got serious, that he could deliver her to ecstasy.

After Amp finished the private dance for the woman in red, he mingled with some other women throughout the club until it was closing time.

"Yo, Dime," Amp called out as the DJ passed by him. He wanted to make sure he saw her before he left, but she kept strutting on by.

He rushed to catch up with her. "I need to settle up with you." That stopped Dime in her tracks. Amp sensed that Dime had a slight attitude for some reason, but he chalked it up to it being the end of a long night.

"Here you go." Amp handed Dime some money. "Thanks again."

"You're welcome." She looked down at the money, folded it, and then tucked it in her pocket. She looked up at Amp. Even if she had been a little salty with him, what woman in her right mind could stay mad at a face like that?

"Hey, you two," Madam said as she walked up to them. Putting a hand on each of their shoulders, she said, "I was thinking we should have a drink to celebrate Mr. Black Magic."

Amp visibly tensed up. "No, thanks. I've gotta get going." He was not about to miss curfew, and he definitely didn't want a drink.

"Suit yourself." Madam shrugged.

"I'm not trying to be rude," Amp said. "It's just—"

She held up a hand to stop him. "No need to explain. But listen, I have a few more high-dollar friends coming this weekend to see my new star," Madam told him. "Don't let me down, okay?"

"I won't," he promised.

Chapter 18

Amp was walking on the outer edge of the parking lot toward his home. It was late, so there wasn't a lot of traffic; just a car here and there rolling by. As Amp was about to cross the street, he looked up and saw the same dark-colored car with tinted windows that he'd seen outside Mr. Lam's store the day after the robbery. Just as Amp was about to step off the curb, another vehicle pulled right up in front of him and stopped. Amp watched cautiously as the car window rolled down.

"Oh my! It's Black Magic!" Dime squealed, throwing her hands up in the air.

Amp laughed with her, watching her overdramatic impression of an ecstatic fan. "Whatever. You pull over just to heckle me?"

"No, I was going to ask if you wanted a ride."

Amp shrugged. "Why not?" Since she'd taken the time to pull over, it wouldn't hurt to accept the offer. The halfway house was pretty close at this point, so it wasn't likely that he'd be sending her out of her way.

As Amp was opening the door to climb in, he looked up and saw that the dark-colored car was no longer there. He wasn't sure how he felt about it. It did seem a little peculiar that the same vehicle had been sort of lurking around—or maybe he was just being paranoid. Years of constantly watching his back was a tough habit to break. He shook it off, getting into Dime's car, and the two took off down the street.

Moments later, Dime pulled into the driveway of the halfway house and put the car in park.

"So . . . you live here?" she asked Amp.

"Yep," he answered, short and sweet. He knew she was just trying to make conversation, but he didn't feel the need to go into details.

The way Dime sat there looking at Amp, it was obvious she expected him to continue, but that was not about to happen. Amp was a private person who minded his own business and expected folks to stay out of his just the same.

There was an awkward silence between them. Neither one was talking, yet Amp wasn't hurrying out of the car. Though he'd spent only a little bit of time in her presence, there was something about this woman that Amp liked.

Finally Dime spoke. "I don't know what's still open. You hungry? Because I'm starving." She obviously liked Amp's company as well.

Amp checked his watch. It was 2:55 a.m., only five minutes before his curfew. Now, back in the joint there might have been occasions where he scarfed down a meal in five minutes, but it wouldn't exactly make a good impression on Dime if he tried to do it tonight.

"Not really," Amp replied to make a long story short—or more like to keep the long story to himself. In truth, he was pretty hungry after dancing and showing out for the past few hours . . . and he definitely wouldn't have minded sharing a meal with Dime. "But if you're around in the morning, we can grab a late breakfast."

Besides, Amp thought, *breakfast is a better first date, because everyone knows dinner always ends with dessert.* He wanted to take his time with Dime. Something about her seemed special, and he wanted to treat her that way.

Dime nodded, nervously tucking a lock of hair behind her ear. "Sounds good. What time?"

"Ten."

"I'll see you then."

Amp opened the door. "Thanks again. Hope you didn't have to go too far outta your way."

"I stay ten minutes from here. No big deal. See you tomorrow."

"All right." Amp got out of the car and walked into the house as Dime drove away. He couldn't wait until morning . . . for more reasons than one.

At ten on the dot the next morning, Dime was back at the house to scoop up Amp.

"Where to?" Amp asked Dime when he got into the car.

"What do you have a taste for?"

"I'm good with whatever," Amp told her. "You're the driver. You decide."

Dime thought for a moment then said, "I know just the spot." She put the car in reverse and backed out of the driveway. "But first things first."

"What do you mean?" Amp asked.

"You'll see. Trust me."

"Trust you, huh?" Amp laughed.

"Yeah, trust me. You got a problem with trusting people . . . or just females?"

"Nope," Amp was quick to say. "Got no problems trusting anybody who earns it."

"Okay, I feel you on that." Dime nodded.

Dime drove for about five more minutes before pulling up at a Bank of America.

"Here we are," she said, turning off the ignition.

"Since when does B of A serve pancakes?"

"They don't," Dime said. "But you're gonna need someplace to put all your money, because I can't keep it every night, Mr. Stripper-man." She smiled at him.

"I hear you. I hear you," he said happily.

"Go ahead. I'll wait out here while you go in and open an account."

Amp nodded, opening the door. Before he stepped out, he said to Dime, "Good looking out." Her thoughtfulness had definitely taken him by surprise. He was so used to being alone and on his own. It was refreshing to have someone looking out for him for a change.

Amp headed inside the bank. Fifteen minutes later, he returned and the two drove off to grab breakfast.

"Thanks for stopping by the bank so I could set up that savings account," Amp said as he and Dime sat in the restaurant eating and talking. "I was getting a little nervous walking around with all that money."

"I bet." Dime took a bite of her pancakes.

"You should have seen their faces in that bank when I pulled out all them damn ones."

Dime laughed, and Amp caught himself watching the way Dime's lips spread into a perfect arch when she laughed. He looked away quickly. If she caught him staring at her, she might take things the wrong way. Yeah, shorty was a cutie, but Amp wasn't trying to start anything serious right now.

Still, he couldn't resist asking, "So how many of the dancers at Eden have asked you out?"

She finished a mouthful of food, looking up at the ceiling as if counting in her head. "All of them, pretty much—but I never went out with any of them. Like I told you, I don't date dancers."

"So, why me?" Amp set his fork down and leaned back against the seat to listen.

"Why you? This ain't a date. This is just breakfast."

Amp smiled, not sure if he should be offended or relieved. "Oh, okay." He leaned back, picked his fork up, and resumed his meal.

Dime said, "If you don't mind me asking, who else lives in that house?"

Knowing women and how curious they were about everything, Amp was willing to bet Dime had been wondering about that since dropping him off last night. Surely she didn't expect that he lived alone in a house that size. Amp figured the real reason she was asking was to make sure a wife and kids weren't waiting for him in that house. If she didn't date dancers, then no doubt she wouldn't date a married man either.

As she sat there waiting for a response, he decided to just go for it and tell her the truth. After all, they weren't on a date, so it wasn't like he had to try to impress her. If his truth turned her off, then so be it.

"It's a long story," Amp offered with a sigh. "Here's the short version: I did a little time. Don't ask me for what. That's a halfway house that I live in. I'm on parole. That's the only reason I started dancing. Need to get my money right so I can get a place and a car. Go back to college." He gave her an I-have-told-you-all-that-I'm-going-to look and then quickly turned the table. "That's my story. What's yours?"

Amp discovered that he felt much better now that he'd told her the truth about his situation. He still had regrets that he had not told Mr. Lam sooner, and he did not want to make the same mistake again, especially with someone who might turn out to be a good friend . . . or more.

To Amp's relief, she didn't press him for any more details. She also didn't hesitate to answer his question. "Well, I used to dance on the other side of Eden back when it had another owner. Needed money for school once my student aid ran out. I heard Madam was purchasing the building, and she had heard I was a good DJ. They needed a female DJ on the men's side, so she hired me. It's a perfect situation. I still make good money, and I get to keep my clothes on."

Amp looked at her through squinted eyes. "Wait, how you gonna say you don't date dancers and you used to strip?"

"I know what that life is all about," she said. "I don't want to have to deal with that."

"I feel you." Amp could only imagine all the emotions one has to go through when dating a dancer, foremost being jealousy.

Dime fell silent and picked at her pancakes with her fork, as if she'd lost her appetite.

"You're all right," Amp said. "I thought you were just some pretty chick that played records. Guess I was wrong."

"And I thought you were just some muscle-bound pretty boy," replied Dime. Amp could tell that calling her pretty did not go unnoticed, as he caught the smile she was trying to suppress.

Amp took one more bite before laying his fork across his plate and wiping his mouth. "Well, Allison, I have to take care of a few things before work tonight, but I think we should do this again sometime."

Dime smiled. "I agree." She took a sip of orange juice. "You need a lift somewhere?"

"Nah. I'm good. Going to look at some apartments." Amp reached into his pocket and pulled out his wallet. He placed enough money on the table to cover the bill and the tip, and then stood up. "I'll see you at work."

"Thanks for breakfast," she said.

"No problem."

Amp walked out of the restaurant wondering if he could make time for a relationship after all. Then he brushed away the thought, telling himself he just didn't have the time. At this moment, it was imperative for him to stay focused. His new life depended on it.

Chapter 19

"I ain't used to being here this early," Dr. Feelgood said, strolling through the club and into Madam's office. "This place looks different during the day."

Madam sat behind her desk, sipping on red wine. She gestured with a nod for Dr. Feelgood to take a seat.

He sat on the other side of the desk. "What'd you need to see me about?"

She set her wine glass down. "Some young lady keeps coming by here looking for you. Today was the third time. You got a stalker or something that you need to let me know about?" He was one of her best dancers, and if there was some kind of problem, she wanted to nip it in the bud before it affected her business.

"Not that I know of."

Madam stared at him momentarily to see if he wanted to add anything else. When he remained quiet, she opened her desk drawer and pulled out a handful of envelopes, laying them down on the desk in front of Dr. Feelgood.

She leaned back in her chair and took another sip of wine.

He sat there staring at the envelopes until she said, "What are you waiting for? Take a look." Then he leaned forward and started flipping through the pile.

"I'm pretty sure that she's the one that's been leaving these letters addressed to you as well," Madam said.

He picked up one of the envelopes with a puzzled expression on his face. "I don't know who this girl is," he told Madam. "And I don't know anything about these letters."

"Initially I thought it was just fan mail, so I wasn't going to bother you about it. But the letters kept coming." Madam picked up the whole pile and handed it to Dr. Feelgood. "Now they're your problem."

He took the stack of letters, paused for a moment, and then leaned over and dropped them in the trash. He looked to Madam. "Anything else?"

"No, but you know my policy, Doc. No drama and no nonsense at my club. I won't have anything up here interfering with my money." Madam always told her dancers that she expected them to control their wives, girlfriends, fiancées, mistresses, side chicks, or whatever. She wanted her customers to know that they could come out and have a good time without one of the dancers' baby mamas going upside their head.

"Yes, ma'am," he said as he stood up and left the office.

Madam returned to her wine and started flipping through a pile of her own mail. Coming across a certified letter marked *URGENT*, she opened it and began reading.

"Wait—there's gotta be some kind of mistake," she said aloud as she stopped to reread the line that had taken her by surprise. Without finishing the rest of the letter, she set the document on her desk and picked up her cell phone.

Scrolling through her contacts, she found the number she was looking for and then pressed *Call*. "Damn it!" she spat when her call was sent to voice mail. She was irritated and anxious to get to the bottom of things.

She looked at the certified letter again and dialed the contact number listed at the bottom. After a couple rings, a receptionist picked up.

"Hi, can I speak to Lisa Howard please?" she said and was quickly placed on hold.

"I'm the owner of Club Eden," she started when Lisa Howard came on the line. Madam was trying to maintain her composure amidst her confusion and frustration. "I got a rather disturbing letter from your office today. There must be some kind of error in your records. . . ." Madam relayed the details of the letter.

As she listened to Lisa Howard's response, all the blood drained from Madam's face. She felt rattled and anxious, and began pacing back and forth. Trying to calm her nerves, she sat on the edge of her desk and guzzled a large gulp of wine. With her back to the door, she didn't see Amp step into the doorway.

"Well, there has to be a way to fix this," she said, continuing her call. "Fine. I'm on the way down there now."

Madam hung up the phone and stood momentarily, with the wine glass in her hands, trembling. She drained the remaining liquid from the glass and then set it down on the desk, hard. As she poured more wine, she looked up to see Amp standing there and then immediately tried to collect herself. She began to pat her hair nervously, which was unusual because she never had a hair out of place.

"What do you need, Amp?" she asked him hurriedly. She needed to go take care of business, sooner rather than later.

"Um, one of the big girls from that birthday group last night tore my thong off of me. I was gonna grab a couple new ones," Amp told her without making eye contact. He was clearly uncomfortable seeing her this way.

"Are you okay?" he asked, being uncharacteristically forward.

Madam nodded her head, struggling to be strong. She even tried to force a slight smile, but it was no use. Amp's worried expression let her know that she wasn't fooling anyone. "No, I'm not," she admitted. "I just got some really bad news and I have to figure out how to fix this."

Madam took another gulp of her wine. "I'm going over there," she said, gathering the certified letter and her purse, and throwing back the last bit of red wine.

Amp went over and started rummaging through the box of outfits, but his mind was obviously still on his boss's atypical behavior. "You know, I'm not doing anything this afternoon. With your nerves being bad and that red wine in you, it might be best if I drive you where you're going."

Madam only hesitated for a second before she tossed him the keys. Who knew? She just might need backup.

Chapter 20

Amp sat in the car, waiting for Madam to exit the county government building. She'd been in there for nearly an hour by the time he finally saw her coming out. She was stoic, wearing a strong front on her face as she made her way to the car. Amp got out and opened the passenger door for her.

She settled into her seat, looking straight ahead. There was no eye contact between them, and no "Thank you for waiting." She was silent. Amp stole a quick glance at her. He saw her eyelids fluttering, and he knew she was fighting off tears. Had she spoken, her voice probably would have cracked.

Amp wanted to ask what was bothering her, but he wasn't sure how to go about it. He didn't want to overstep his boundaries and have her think that he was snooping in her business. If she'd wanted him to know all the details, then she would have told him. So instead, he said nothing. He just started the car.

Her emotions got the best of her, and Madam turned her face toward the window as a tear ran down her face. Amp had to ask her what was going on at this point. He couldn't just drive down the street with a crying woman and show no concern at all.

"Is it something that you can talk about?" Amp shifted the car in drive, leaving his foot on the brake.

Madam was quiet for a moment, but she looked over to Amp and saw the genuine concern on his face. "There's . . . a really good chance—" She paused to wipe a tear that rolled down her cheek. "I'm going to end up losing my club." She shook her head as the dam broke and the tears came harder. She'd tried so hard to maintain her composure and keep her dignity, but Amp recognized that she'd dedicated her life to building her business, so even the possibility of a loss must have been incredibly painful for her.

"I worked so hard to have something of my own. And now this . . ." she cried.

Amp knew what it was like to lose everything, so he could relate to her pain. "Is there anything that the rest of us can do to help?" he offered.

Madam shook her head.

"Look, I get the 'I'm strong and I can do it by myself' thing, I do, but you have a whole team of people that can help—if you just tell us how."

She didn't answer him, so he just sat there for a while as her tears continued to roll. Sometimes a good cry was what a person needed, to just let it all out.

Amp started thinking about all of the times he'd felt desperate and wished someone had been there for him. He was determined to help Madam now. He tried again to reassure her. "No matter how bad it looks, you don't strike me as the type of person that's just gonna give up."

She still didn't answer, so he decided he'd better give her some space. He would try again later to get her to talk.

Amp drove himself back to the halfway house with no conversation taking place between him and Madam. After he was sure that she had calmed down enough to drive, he turned her keys over to her.

"Madam," he said before getting out of the car, "you know you can call me if you need anything." He would be there for her. After all, she had given him a chance, and Amp was loyal to those that were there for him.

When Amp arrived back at Club Eden later that night, it wasn't opened for the public yet. El

Fuego, Babyface, and Casanova were talking by the bar.

"What's going on, Amp?" Casanova greeted.

"Same stuff, different day," Amp replied, giving him dap.

"Check it out," El Fuego said with a slight Latin accent. Whenever he was hollering at the ladies, he always had his accent on level ten. There was just something about the women hearing his deep Latin accent that made them really go into their purses. "These rich chicks hired me to do a private party for them this weekend. They saw your act last week and asked me to bring you along. It's two stacks, plus tips, for two hours."

"Damn." Amp's eyes dang near popped out. "They paying you that kind of money, you gon' have to bang them rich old broads."

"I'm gonna make three or four grand in two hours, my friend. I don't care." He said it and he meant it. Everyone knew El Fuego was in a bind similar to Amp's. On top of having to cover his own monthly expenses, he was sending money back home to Mexico to help his family. He had a huge family, and within the Latin culture it's family first, so El Fuego was not above occasionally putting it on a woman or two at the private parties for some extra money. The rest of the guys never acted like they knew about it. It was his business.

"I'm good, bro." Amp shook his head then looked to Casanova. "Cass, you going?"

"Nope," he replied without hesitation. "I don't do private parties."

"Why not?" Amp asked.

"Well . . . I, uh . . ." Casanova stammered. He couldn't get the words out, so El Fuego answered for him.

"He's super religious."

"I am not," Casanova said.

"You repent, pray, and say ten *Hail Marys* after each dance." El Fuego laughed.

"So what? I'm asking for forgiveness," Casanova said, straightening the cross pendant on his necklace.

El Fuego raised his hands in surrender. "I'm not judging you. I just think it's hilarious that one minute you're in the locker room quoting scriptures, and the next minute you're out here with a Zorro outfit on."

Amp and Babyface busted out laughing, but Casanova did not look amused.

"Fellas, listen up," Madam said as she eagerly entered the bar area, interrupting their conversation. "I need all of you guys in my office now." She didn't even wait for a response as she kept walking right on by them, the sound of her heels clicking all the way into her office.

The guys gave each other questioning looks as they followed behind her.

"Not you, Babyface," Madam said as she settled in behind her desk.

Babyface stopped in his tracks and held his hands up in wonderment. "Am I in trouble?"

"No," Madam said. "I need you to take care of something. One of your women is making a scene in my parking lot. She's out there right now tearing up your car and singing."

His face twisted up in confusion. "Singing?" he asked just as everyone heard the sound of shattering glass. Babyface ran outside the club. Everyone else stayed put for a second, but as the noise escalated, Madam decided to forgo her impromptu meeting.

"Maybe you all should follow him out there, just in case," she said.

Out in the parking lot, Babyface yelled, "Valerie! What are you doing?"

"I bust the windows out your car. . . ." Valerie was sobbing and singing the song by Jasmine Sullivan at the same time. She wore a T-shirt with pajama pants and fluffy house shoes, and her messy hair was sticking to the tears on her face. She didn't look like a woman who was in her right mind. The bat she was using to bust the headlights on Babyface's black Dodge Charger completed the picture of a woman gone mad.

Babyface approached his car, keeping a safe distance from Valerie so that she didn't knock his lights out as well. Ol' girl kept singing and swinging.

"Valerie, stop!" he shouted.

She stopped momentarily to look at Babyface through her red, puffy eyes. "Why should I?" Valerie sobbed. "You around here messing with other chicks, driving them around in the car I bought you! I pay the note on this car, so I can tear it up if I want to."

"Val, please. I don't know what you're talking about. I—"

"Don't you dare patronize me!" Valerie snapped. "I know what my eyes saw, but just in case, I captured it on my cell phone camera too. You wanna see?"

This was not a joke. Valerie was really busting up his car, which must have meant she really had hardcore evidence against him.

Valerie raised the bat to hit the car again, and Babyface stepped closer. He couldn't just stand back and let her demolish his ride.

She turned her attention to Babyface and shrieked, "You might as well have just stabbed me in the stomach with a knife. I've never felt this kind of hurt, because I've never loved any man as I loved you." Her pain was obviously intense. "How could you throw away two years? How could you do this to me?"

She started walking slowly toward him with the bat now gripped in both hands. It was positioned behind her head as if she were ready to hit a homerun.

Amp decided it was time to intervene. He was thinking about the best way to try to get the bat away from her. She had clearly snapped, and Amp knew all too well that this could end badly.

"Stop!"

Everyone turned in the direction of the voice to find Madam walking toward them.

"The police will be here in two minutes," Madam told Valerie. "So if you don't want to go to jail tonight, you better get out of here."

Madam's statements must have registered with Valerie, because she slowly lowered the bat. She looked to Babyface, back to Madam, and then headed toward her car, dragging the bat on the ground.

Pausing in front of Babyface's car for a moment, she swung the bat one more time. Babyface cringed as the last headlight exploded.

"We'll talk about this when I get home tonight. Okay, babe?" he said in a sugary voice.

Valerie didn't respond. She simply threw the bat into her car, got in, and drove away, giving Babyface the look of death as she passed him.

"You're gonna end up on *Snapped* if you go home to her tonight," Madam said, watching the madwoman drive away. "That girl's gonna kill you."

"You're right," he acknowledged. "And thanks for saving me."

"I had to. She was wasting my time, and I couldn't start this meeting without you and the guys. Come on." She waved her hand, signaling for everyone to come back inside.

This was the first time since Amp started working there that he had been called to a meeting. He wondered if it had anything to do with that trip to the government office earlier.

Madam sat down at her desk, took a sip of her signature red wine, and then got straight to the point. "The bottom line is I may lose this building."

The men were speechless as they stared at Madam, waiting for her to continue. She said nothing else, though. Clearly it had been hard enough for her to admit that much.

"I thought you owned it." Dr. Feelgood had a puzzled look on his face.

"I do," Madam confirmed. "Apparently my accountant—actually, ex-accountant—hasn't been paying the property taxes on this building. He kept the money I gave him to do so, and now no one can find him. So, long story short, unless I can come up with that money, the county is going to seize the building and sell it to pay the back taxes."

Babyface spoke next. "Exactly how much money are we talking about? And how much time?"

"I have sixty days to pay them two hundred and fifty thousand dollars," Madam said.

"Dayum," was the general reaction to the amount owed and the short amount of time she had to pay the debt.

Silence fell over the room for a moment, until Casanova folded his hands together and said, "We need to pray."

"Cass, this ain't the time," El Fuego said.

"There is always time for Jesus! Always!" Casanova was adamant.

Madam calmly took a sip of her wine. "You can pray for us later, Cass. Right now, let's focus."

"Is that even possible?" Amp questioned. "To make that kind of money in sixty days?"

Madam shook her head. "I don't know, but we're going to damn sure try. I have a little bit saved up, so that should help, but we are going to have to pull some money together and fast. Now, this won't affect the money you make at all. I know y'all need this place as much as I do, so I am going to need everyone's help."

Madam stood and began pacing as she ran down the game plan to her players. "We're going to have to pull double and triple duty some days, meaning two events, and sometimes three, per day."

No one spoke up to disagree, so Madam continued. "Also, I want to do a big exotic auction featuring you guys. It'll be a great way to raise some money, and I can bring in some of your high-dollar customers for that event. And if any of you have any ideas, feel free to share. This is going to take all of us to pull this off."

Dr. Feelgood looked up, and his eyes landed on the calendar on the wall. "We could do a calendar, and all the money we raise can go toward the club," he suggested.

"That's a good idea," Amp agreed. Although he hadn't been around as long as the other dancers, he had developed a true respect for Madam. From the moment he'd met her in the park, he'd admired her business sense. And, of course, he also appreciated the fact that she put him on, even if it did mean her insurance would go up a little. She gave him a chance.

"While we're out selling the calendars," Amp contributed, "we can promote the auction."

"That could work," Madam agreed.

"It's going to have to!" El Fuego said matter-of-factly. "I need this job."

"We all do," Babyface said.

Madam checked the time. "Doors open in thirty minutes. Let's have a great night."

Babyface, El Fuego, and Casanova started to file out of the room while Amp went to the cabinet to find an outfit, since he hadn't had time that afternoon. With the bomb Madam just dropped on them, it was going to be hard to have a great night, but business was business. Once they hit that stage, they had to leave their personal lives behind and focus on business—even if the threat of losing the club made it personal.

"Face," Madam called out.

Babyface turned to Madam as the other men headed out.

"Clean up that mess your psycho girlfriend made in the parking lot, before the club opens."

"I'm on it," Babyface replied.

"And don't let it happen again."

"Yes, ma'am."

Babyface exited the office, and Madam went back over to her desk to finish her wine and get started on some paperwork.

Amp quickly found something to wear and turned to leave, not wanting to disturb Madam.

"Amp," she said, looking up from her paperwork.

Standing in the doorway, he turned to face her.

"Thank you."

Amp nodded. "You're welcome."

A short while later, things were back to business as Dr. Feelgood took the stage as the opening act for the night. One eager woman was pulled from the audience and laid on his stretcher, while Dr. Feelgood used his upper body strength to do a dance over her without their bodies ever touching. Both hands planted above her shoulders, his left leg planted beside her right, he butterflied his right leg as if he were grinding her. From the audience's view, it looked as if the woman could possibly leave the stage pregnant, but Dr. Feelgood had managed to come just close enough to her where she could feel only the heat of his body.

Next to take the stage was Casanova. Although eighty-five percent of the audience was African American women who generally preferred their

men darker, five seconds of admiring this spec-
imen had them ready to play in the snow. The
way they saw it, he had good credit, was always
on time, and he could move like he grew up
in the hood. What was hotter than that? He
had the ladies going crazy, especially when he
blessed one with the privilege of removing the
single rose that rested in his mouth with her
own mouth.

Once El Fuego hit the stage and did his Latin-
themed show, the women were fit to be tied. In
all the excitement, the audience started yelling
random Spanish words that they probably
couldn't even translate.

The best had been saved for last, when Amp
killed his routine. He could just sweep the room
with his eyes and have the women lose control.
With him, it was his demeanor and swag.

"Take it all!" a woman yelled, throwing her
whole clutch full of money on stage while Amp
was dancing. Amp would laugh about it later,
but right now he had work to do. The club was
at stake.

There was one woman in particular—or one
who mattered the most to him—who was mesmerized by how smooth Amp was on the stage. It
was Dime. As Amp moved stage right, he could
feel Dime staring at him in his peripheral vision.

He liked knowing that he turned her on but that she was staying cool about hers. If Amp was going to make a move, he would have to take the lead. He hadn't decided if he would, but he liked that Dime wasn't thirsty and gave him the time to choose.

Amp's song was ending, and it was time for Dime to put on a new song. Amp smiled at her for a brief second before he got back in the zone and took his dancing up another notch.

Chapter 21

"You have arrived at your final destination," the GPS told El Fuego as he pulled into the driveway of the home in Woodland Hills, where he'd been hired to do a private party. He cracked a smile when he saw the beautiful, enormous home. A big house meant big money and big tips.

"Oh, great. It's one of those," El Fuego said as it dawned on him that there were no other cars in the driveway or parked on the street in front of the house. Typically, when he was told to be there early, he was asked to hide in some back room and pop out to surprise all the guests when they arrived. "I just hope it's not another cake," he complained.

He turned off the car, grabbed his duffle bag, and headed for the door. The doorbell played a ten-second serenade, but there was no answer.

He backed up and looked at the numbers on the house. They matched the address she'd given him over the phone, so he was definitely at the right place, although now he noticed that the house was pretty dimly lit for a party about to take place. He pulled out his cell phone and checked the time: eight o'clock sharp, just like she'd said.

El Fuego rang the doorbell again, telling himself that if he didn't get an answer this time, he was out. A few seconds passed and once again, there was no answer. El Fuego shrugged: *Oh, well. I tried.*

Just as he turned around to leave, the door cracked open and he saw a woman standing there in a plain, black, En Vogue–slinky, form-fitting dress.

"Karen?" El Fuego asked. He knew nothing about the woman who'd hired him, other than her first name and the fact that she'd been referred to him by one of her girlfriends.

"El Fuego?" she said.

"Yes."

She smiled and sensually extended her hand, looking him up and down from head to toe. "My girlfriend was right. You are perfect for the job." She opened the door all the way, moving to the side to let him enter.

El Fuego stepped into the marble-floored foyer as Karen closed and locked the door behind them. "Nice place you got here. Those chandeliers—" He pointed to the double crystal chandeliers hanging from the vaulted ceiling. "Nice." He was no home designer or anything like that, but he took note of nice things. Besides that, he knew women loved compliments. It made them happy, which meant they were more generous with their tips.

"Thank you. My husband does all the decorating," Karen said, standing there looking at him like she could eat him alive.

"Well, your husband has great taste, I must say." El Fuego returned his slick, intentional double entendre and gave her the once over she'd given him earlier.

Now that she was no longer partially covered by the door, he could fully take in all her thickness. She was a solid and curvy perfect size twelve.

"Thank you." She blushed, sweeping her short bobbed hairstyle behind her ear.

There was a moment of silence before El Fuego asked, "Well, is there someplace I can change before everybody else gets here?"

Karen looked puzzled. "Everybody else? Did you invite someone?"

Now El Fuego was the one who was confused. "When you called you said you needed me to dance for a private party. I assumed it was for a group of your girlfriends."

"I don't know where you're from, but I don't need a houseful of people to make a party," she said with a wink.

"So, wait a minute. There is no one else? Just me and you?"

"Is that a problem?" she said coyly.

"I mean, what about your husband?" El Fuego was not trying to get caught up in any jealous husband drama. He'd witnessed enough of that going down at the club, and at least there they had security. He was now on someone else's turf.

"Oh, no. He doesn't get down like that. It will just be the two of us," she said so nonchalantly that El Fuego got the impression that she and her husband had an "understanding."

She walked closer to El Fuego, and he took a step back. "What if he comes home and finds a half-naked man dancing on his wife?" He shook his head and waved his hands. He definitely wasn't comfortable with this.

"Look, Karen, you're a sexy, lovely-looking woman, and what you're willing to pay me is more than I could even—"

"You're right. There is a risk factor involved for you that I didn't think about before, so I'll double it."

El Fuego struggled to keep his mouth from dropping open. This woman had already agreed to pay him two thousand dollars, and now she was talking about doubling it to four. Any other time he might have had his doubts, but from the looks of that home and that designer dress she was wearing, which was probably tailor made to fit her curves, she was definitely good for the money. This was no joke. Ol' girl was serious about how she'd planned for her Saturday night to go down—and who was he to ruin a girl's plans?

"Is that a yes?" Karen asked. "The fact that you haven't walked out that door yet?"

El Fuego repeated, "Like I said before: Is there someplace I can change?"

Karen gave him a huge grin, pointing down the hallway. "Right that way."

El Fuego entered a half bathroom that was the size of two full baths in a regular house, and he proceeded to change into a red thong with sheer black boxers and a sheer black robe. Barefoot, he exited the bathroom and saw that Karen was no longer standing in the foyer. The chandeliers were no longer lit.

"Karen?" he called out.

"I'm in here," she replied, her voice coming from the direction of a dim, flickering light.

El Fuego entered the great room to find several candles lighting the space. The fireplace was burning, purely for ambiance, because God knows it was already hot in there.

Sitting in a chair in front of the fireplace was Karen, legs crossed. Her arms were crossed, and her hands were resting on her knees. She was patiently waiting.

"Isn't this how you all do it?" she asked seductively. "You place the woman in a chair and then lavish her, and only her, with all of your attention?"

El Fuego licked his lips. "Something like that." He began to untie his robe as he walked toward her.

"Oh, wait! I forgot music. How could I be so—" She got out of the chair, but El Fuego placed his hands gently on her shoulders before she could move.

"Uh-uh." He shook his head. "I'll turn the music on. I don't need this chair, though."

She watched as he lifted the chair with one hand and set it in the corner. On his way back to Karen, he pressed play on her iPod, and the Bose surround sound system filled the room with the sexiest of sounds. Miguel's "Adorn" would set the mood for them that night.

"What do you want me to do?" she asked.

"Nothing," El Fuego said, brushing his lips against her ear and making the hairs on her neck rise. "I'm going to do everything." He slowly walked around her until he was standing in front, tracing her spine with his hand the entire way. "Isn't that what you're paying me to do?" He looked her up and down. "But I'm sure you know how to work it." He shook his head at all she was working with indeed.

By now, Karen was speechless as El Fuego stood in front of her, placed his hands on her shoulders, and began to gyrate his body in front of her while staring in her eyes.

With his robe swinging open, Karen placed her hands on his waist so she could feel the waves in the ocean rolling. She tightened her grip, unable to resist the feel of his hard body.

As El Fuego's body swayed, he lowered himself to his knees and then lifted one of Karen's legs and ran his face down her thigh, just barely touching her. In one swift motion, he'd lifted her other leg and had her sitting on his shoulders.

"Oh, my!" she said in surprise. She hadn't been expecting that at all. Karen was no tiny chick, either, standing five feet nine inches. How this man managed to keep her there while still waving his body, she had no idea. He wasn't even trembling as if he were struggling with her weight. No, he continued his body movements, now adding neck motion as his head danced between her legs.

Slowly El Fuego leaned back. He got lower and lower to the ground as if he were a contortionist. Positioning Karen on her knees, his face still buried between her legs, he blew hot breath on her, teasing her clit. Suddenly, a slight pressure made her think that he was pressing up against her with his tongue.

He managed to slide out from underneath her, leaving her on her knees, facing away from him. Her dress was flipped up and her butt cheeks were hanging out.

"I see somebody else likes thongs too," El Fuego whispered in her ear then smacked her ass. He mumbled something else she didn't understand in his native tongue, but that Latin accent—not to mention that hard Latin body—made her want to take up Spanish. She wanted to be able to talk that talk as well. Right now, though, they were both speaking the same language: lust.

Karen's thoughts vanished when El Fuego slid his head underneath her and then lifted her up onto his shoulders. When he spun her around his neck so that her crotch was now in his face, she felt like emptying her entire bank account for this man.

"Oh, God!" This time she was sure that his tongue was pressing up against her throbbing clit.

"No, you can just call me El Fuego," he teased, dropping her off his neck and then catching her effortlessly by the waist. He began doing a grinding dance that made her body go limp. It was as if they were on the erotic version of *Dancing with the Stars,* and Karen was partnered with the award-winning star.

Things only got more intense from there. El Fuego worked his way between her legs, and damn, he was a perfect fit!

Three orgasms later, Karen couldn't take any more. Plus, she had to wrap things up and clean up before her husband got home. She happily paid El Fuego and sent him on his way. He would definitely be returning for another private party very soon.

Chapter 22

This time when Dime dropped Amp off at the halfway house, he wasn't in a hurry to beat curfew. He had about twenty minutes to spare instead of five, so the two stepped outside the car and chopped it up. Amp and Dime were side by side, leaned up against her car in the driveway.

"So, when you get out of here and get your own place,"—She nodded toward the house—"are you going to keep dancing?"

"Good question." Amp stared off into the night. "I'm not sure. I don't want to. I'd rather get a regular job." He folded his arms and looked to Dime. "What about you? How long are you going to keep DJ'ing at a strip club?"

"Not long. I'm looking for a good job in my field, then I'm outta there." Dime shared with Amp that she had graduated from college with a degree in business and finance. "The money from my other job isn't enough to make ends meet, so until I find something that pays better, I have to keep DJ'ing at night."

Amp was surprised. "Word? You have another job?"

"I have a part-time accounting job during the day, which bores me to death." Dime let her head fall to the side, closed her eyes, and fake snored. "But it pays the bills. Student loans." She shook her head.

Amp looked down at his wrist and realized that he wasn't wearing his watch. He must have left it in his locker back at the club. "What time is it?"

Dime pulled out her cell phone and checked the time. "Ten minutes to three," she told him.

"I have to go in a second." He wished he could stand out there all night and talk to Dime. If he wasn't mistaken, that guard she had up had lowered—and Dime could easily say the same about him.

"You want to grab breakfast in the morning?" she asked.

"Can't. I have to do some chores around here in the morning. I can do lunch though."

Dime smiled. "Lunch it is."

"You sure can do breakfast and lunch a lot to have a day job."

"Part-time, remember."

Amp stood up off of the car, unfolding his arms. "I need to get a cell phone and a couple outfits tomorrow, so let's eat somewhere close to the mall."

"Okay."

Amp gave Dime an authentic but slightly uncomfortable hug and walked toward the house. It had been a while since he had been so close to a woman that he was kind of feeling. Private dances at the club were the only up close and personal interaction Amp had received in a while, and none of those women kept his attention beyond the dollar bills they were dropping.

Amp had been a free spirit before he went to prison. Back then he'd dated plenty of girls, but he was never looking for anything serious, just a drama-free good time. He could see that with Dime, things were different. She wasn't the type that a man could have a casual relationship with. She was the kind of chick a man made his woman. He wondered if he was ready for that kind of grown-man, "Barack and Michelle" kind of love and commitment.

Amp was really contemplating the idea, though. Dime had proven to have brains plus beauty, and above all she had his back—not because he was "breaking her back" but because she seemed to genuinely care for his wellbeing. She could really be the one.

"See you tomorrow," Amp said, grinning.

"Good night," Dime said as she watched him walk up the steps onto the porch. Amp turned and waved then went inside.

It had been a long day. He went straight up to his bedroom, took a hot shower, and then got into bed, where he fell asleep almost instantly. Snoring deeply, Amp began to dream, but it wasn't his usual nightmare. Instead, this dream was about Dime, and she was calling him Black Magic over and over and over again. . . .

Just the sound of Amp's stage name rolling off her tongue excited Dime as every inch of him was inside of her. The same way Amp was rough around the edges in everyday life, he was rough when it came to sexing her up, and she loved it. Her legs bounced in the air with each pounding thrust.

Amp let out a moan that reflected both pleasure and pain, like he was mad at the world and was taking it out on her kitten. But it hurt so good for Dime, as she purred contentedly with each and every stroke.

Pouring with sweat, Amp raised up over her on his arms like he was doing push-ups. His upper body remained stiff and hard as he worked his lower part deep into her.

Unashamed, Dime called out his name repeatedly as she tried to keep up with him and throw her hips right back at him. It was useless; she couldn't keep up. He was releasing years of pent-up sexual energy, and she was glad to be on the receiving end. She rested her bottom on the bed and let Amp do what he did, which was hit every sweet spot inside her sugar walls. As she ran her hands up and down his back, she could feel every muscle popping out of his back.

Every so often Amp would become gentle, slowly pulling himself out of her, and then he'd ram himself inside again, then hold it there. He knew that was the spot from the way her nails sliced at his back. He was giving it to her like he loved her and hated her at the same time, and she loved it.

Dime opened wide and wrapped her long, sexy legs around him. Being inside her felt so good to Amp that it almost hurt.

Propped up on the pillow, Dime looked over Amp's shoulders and watched his ass while he went in and out of her. The simple fact that he was still wearing the same black military boots that he danced in made her cum. Her lady muscle tightened around Amp as she released, then relaxed her muscle, ready for him to get her off again. The way he was going at it, she knew he wasn't done.

A sensation aroused in Dime that she had never experienced before as she not only climaxed a second time, but she squirted. Her eyes shot open toward the ceiling because for a minute there she thought she was peeing. That's just how crazy it felt. It was almost like an out of body experience. She didn't even know her kitten was capable of squirting milk. She closed her eyes as Amp reached his climax.

As his legs shook and his core muscle tensed up with every release, Amp awoke to discover that he had been dreaming. His first thought was, *I like her.* He turned over and went back to sleep, hoping that there would be a second act to that dream.

The next morning, Amp was sweeping the sidewalk and cleaning up the front yard when Paul came out of the house to talk to him.

"How's it going?" Paul asked.

"It's going," Amp replied as he bent over to pick up a smashed McDonald's cup off the sidewalk. He placed it in the bag he'd been using to collect trash and twigs then continued to sweep.

"Just curious. . . . You're a free man in about six weeks. What are you going to do then?"

Amp stopped sweeping and gave Paul his attention. "Not sure yet. I've been putting money up and looking at some apartments."

"You got any family around here?" The only thing Paul knew about Amp was what was in his file, which made no mention of his family. The two had never sat down and had a personal conversation.

"Some. But they pretty much turned their backs on me. They stopped taking my calls when I went to prison."

"I'll make some calls and see if I can help with your apartment search. If there's anything else you need help with, let me know."

"I will. Thank you."

As Amp went back to his cleanup work, he reflected on how grateful he was for the people God had sent into his life. Although there were a lot of challenges for him to overcome, he felt he was finally headed in the right direction. Everything would be all right.

Amp got off the city bus and walked a couple of blocks, stopping in front of a building that housed the University of Southern California administrative offices. Being back on this campus brought back a lot of memories for Amp, both good and bad. A smile spread across his lips as he reflected on the good ones: the parties, the music, the laughter with friends.

There was always something fun and crazy going down, and Amp was always a part of it. He was serious about his business, but he really did know how to take the edge off when it came to winding down and relaxing. He enjoyed reliving those memories—until his mind traveled back to the night he'd had a little too much fun. That was the night that changed everything.

The smile on his face was soon replaced with a frown as the sober reality of that night cast a dark cloud over his past and continued to rain on his present. He had to make things right, and being here was the first step.

Taking a deep breath, Amp walked into the building and followed the signs that led him to the front desk of the academic records office. There were a couple of students standing in line, so Amp took his place behind them.

When it was finally Amp's turn, a forty-year-old woman in a navy blue skirt and blazer signaled for him to approach the desk.

"Good afternoon," she greeted Amp. "How can I help you?"

"I need to get a list of the classes I've taken and credit hours I have completed here," Amp told her.

"Okay, so you need a copy of your transcript."

"Yes, ma'am."

The receptionist punched some buttons on her keyboard. "The cost for that is twenty-five dollars."

"Damn. For a piece of paper?" Amp had definitely not been prepared to come off of twenty-five dollars of his savings. It might not have sounded like a lot of money to someone in a different situation, but for Amp every dollar was a step closer toward his independence and future. He had to think about this one, so that's just what he did for the next couple of seconds.

"You want it or not?" the receptionist asked with a hint of impatience.

What choice did Amp really have? He needed the transcript, so if he had to pay twenty-five dollars to get it, what else could he do? "Yes, I want it."

"Name?" she asked.

"Amp Anthony."

She typed his name in the computer, and moments later the transcript printed out. Retrieving it from the printer, she held it in her hands in front of Amp.

"Will that be cash or check?" she asked.

"Cash." Amp handed her the money, and in return she handed him the transcript and a receipt.

"Anything else I can help you with?" she asked.

"Yes, actually." Amp cleared his throat and leaned in a little. Upon instinct the receptionist leaned in too, close enough so that the scent of her perfume flirted with Amp's nose.

"I'm trying to locate someone," he said. "I think she's a student here. Can you check the name Shannon Ellis, please?"

The receptionist typed the name into the computer and waited for the results. Amp was hopeful that it would be more than just a photo, which was all he'd been able to come up with on his search for the name Patricia Ellis.

"Well, it says here that Ms. Shannon Ellis is a graduate student," the receptionist told him, "but I'm not allowed to give you her personal information."

Amp could hardly contain his excitement on hearing the little bit of information the receptionist had decided to share. He leaned into the desk with a look of desperation in his eyes. "Ma'am, it is very important that I talk to her. How about giving me the day and time of one of her classes? I promise, I'm not a stalker or some weirdo. Please." He hoped that she could sense his sincerity as he pleaded with her.

She didn't shut him down immediately, and the look on her face told Amp that she was considering granting his request. Thinking it might help his cause, Amp gave her the smile that few women could resist. He thought he saw the hint of a smirk pass over her face.

"I'm sorry, Mr. Anthony, but I can't give you that information either." While she spoke, she turned her computer screen so that Amp could see all the information on Shannon Ellis. She then placed a piece of paper and a pen on the counter and walked away.

Amp quickly wrote down information from the screen and left. He had what he needed. Now came the hard part.

Chapter 23

It was just a few minutes before the doors would open at Club Eden, and Amp and Babyface were in the stage area, shooting the breeze. Babyface was talking with Amp about a private party he'd done the night before, but there was something more interesting holding Amp's attention. He could hardly maintain eye contact with Babyface, for his attention was traveling off elsewhere—specifically, the DJ booth. Dime had been on his mind quite a bit lately.

"I meant to ask what's up with you and Dime," Babyface said when he noticed how hard Amp was focusing on Dime as she set up for the night. "I see you two getting a little close."

Without taking his eyes off Dime, he answered, "I don't know. We cool. I'm just really starting to get to know her a little better."

Amp couldn't lie to himself, though. There was a part of him that definitely wanted to get to know more about her. She was cool people, had a good head on her shoulders, and was a hard worker like him. She was definitely someone Amp wouldn't mind connecting with on a personal level. The look in his eyes as he stared at her was a dead giveaway of his true feelings.

"I see you." Babyface laughed.

"I'm telling you, it ain't like that—at least not yet."

Dime looked up and caught Amp checking her out.

"See, you starting shit. She prolly heard you." Having made eye contact with Dime, Amp couldn't be rude and not go over there and speak. "I'll get up with you in a minute, man." He dapped Babyface and walked over to the DJ booth.

"You two over there talking about me?" Dime asked Amp as he approached the booth.

"Possibly."

Dime took that as a yes and cracked a smile, trying not to blush. "So, when are you going to stop being so distant with me? I know you like me." Dime looked away from Amp and continued setting up her equipment.

"And I know you like me." Amp wasn't beneath playing along in their flirting session. Now it was Dime's move.

Before she could respond, a woman came rushing out of Madam's office. She looked bound and determined to make it out of that club without being stopped or asked any questions. She kept her eyes and feet straight on the exit path. Seconds later, Madam came out of her office looking pissed.

"Let's pick this up later, love," Amp said to Dime.

"Okay," she agreed. "We'll talk later." They were both looking at Madam to see if she was going to comment on what had just happened.

"Where the hell is Doc?" Madam yelled, fists on hips and chest rising up and down. She was pissed to the tenth power.

"I don't think he's here yet," Dime replied.

"As soon as he gets here, send him in to see me!" Madam stormed back into her office.

Amp and Dime shot each other a look that said they were both glad they weren't in Dr. Feelgood's shoes. Madam was on the warpath, and she had made it clear that he was her target.

No sooner than Madam had slammed her office door behind her, Dr. Feelgood entered the club.

"Yo, Doc," Dime called out. "Madam came out of her office looking for you. And she didn't look too happy."

"Yeah," Amp jumped in. "You better see what she wants before she comes back out—"

"And finds you," Dime said, finishing his sentence.

Their warning was too late. Madam had already come back out and was standing in front of him with a letter in one hand and a baby in tow.

"Someone left this for you."

He grabbed the letter, noticing that it had already been opened. "Okay, thanks."

"No, this." Madam raised up the baby in the carrier so Dr. Feelgood could take a good look. He was absolutely speechless.

"His mama stopped by a little earlier," Madam said, looking down at the baby in his blue onesie with a blue baby cap on his head. "I was on the phone, finishing up a call, so I didn't see her set this child down and walk out." Madam nodded toward the letter in his hand. "But per that letter, looks like this little bundle of joy is yours."

Still, words escaped Dr. Feelgood.

"This is the type of shit I mean when I say don't let your personal lives spill over into my place of business."

Shaking his head, Dr. Feelgood replied, "I don't know anything about this. I don't even know that this baby is really mine." He looked from the letter to the baby, then back to the letter again. This had to be a joke. This couldn't be happening—but the sound of the baby cooing let him know this was very real. That was no baby doll.

"Well, if you had read any of the letters that had been left here for you, you would probably know. She's been trying to contact you about this for a while now. And she's willing to take a DNA test to prove that it's yours—at least according to that letter she is. So, you need to take this baby out of here now." Madam extended the baby to its maybe-daddy.

"And go where?" he asked Madam.

"I don't know, but this isn't a day care center," she told him. "Maybe you should go track down Ms. Alicia and get your life together."

Dr. Feelgood took her advice and walked off, still stunned.

Madam then realized that Dime and Amp had been standing there listening the whole time.

"And you two, get to work," she barked.

Amp and Dime immediately picked up their belongings and kept it moving. The show was over, and it was time for them to get ready for the real show and make that cash.

Chapter 24

It had been yet another great night at Club Eden, for the women and for the dancers. Amp had done especially well.

Once the bartender announced last call, Amp headed to the locker room to get changed. He came back out and did what had become an evening ritual for him: He helped Dime carry her things to her car.

"Now, about our conversation from earlier . . ." Dime said, as if she'd been waiting all night to see where Amp's head was at.

Amp didn't mind. He enjoyed the fact that they were making progress in this . . . thing they had going on. Like he'd told Babyface, he didn't even know if it could be called a relationship, but whatever it was, it was progressing.

"Okay. Here it is then. I'm dealing with some stuff," Amp told her.

"What stuff?"

"I don't go around discussing my life with people—especially people I don't know very well." He stopped what he was doing and looked at Dime with curiosity in his eyes. If whatever was going on between the two of them was headed somewhere, he didn't want to put a halt to it by exposing more information than he needed to. Amp had a feeling, however, that just like him, a part of Dime did want things to go somewhere between them. She hadn't run off yet, even though she knew that he had been in prison.

"And why you want to mess with a guy like me anyway? I'm damaged goods. I'm trying to fix some of these things, but I'm just not there yet."

Dime sucked her teeth, expressing her disappointment with being once again brushed off by Amp.

"I promise, in time, I'll tell you what you need to know," he said.

"Okay, but at least tell me this: Why, when I offer you a ride, do you almost always say no? Is it pride?"

Amp went back to helping Dime load the car. "Yes, partly. I don't want to feel like a charity case. But it's also because after being locked up for a long time, it's nice just to be able to walk anywhere."

"That makes sense," Dime said. "You want a ride?"

Amp smirked. "Why not?"

They loaded the rest of Dime's equipment and got in the car. Like she'd done on a few occasions now, Dime drove Amp home—or at least the place he called home for now. It was only a matter of time before he'd have a place of his own.

After bidding Dime a good night, Amp went in the house, grabbed a plate of leftovers, hit the shower, and then hit the hay. As dog tired as he was, he thought he'd fall into a deep sleep just as soon as his head hit the pillow. He had hoped to dream about making love to Dime again, but that wasn't the case. He was sleeping restlessly, tossing and turning.

He sat up in his bed and looked at the clock. Although it felt like he'd been lying there for hours, it had only been about thirty minutes. Next to the clock lay the newspaper article he was always rereading. He shook his head in frustration at the roller coaster ride that was his life. One minute he was in the car with Dime, feeling like things were moving in the right direction, and then he was in bed, staring at an article that reminded him of the terrible mistake he'd made that put him on this rocky path. Clearly sleep was nowhere in the vicinity of his bedroom, so he got out of bed and headed downstairs.

Amp was creeping through the house as quietly as possible. He went into the kitchen to get a glass of water, and then went into the living room, where he saw Paul in the corner, headphones on, listening to his records. Amp went over and sat on the couch across from him.

Paul took off his headphones. "Can't sleep, huh?"

"Yeah." Amp sipped his water. "You would know a little something about that, wouldn't you?" That was Amp's way of letting Paul know he could talk about what it was that gave him his sleepless nights if he wanted to. Amp would be a listening ear.

"What do you mean by that?"

"It may not be the same thing haunting you, but something keeps you up at night."

"Listen," Paul said. "You focus on getting your shit together. Don't worry about mine." He picked up the headphones again and adjusted them. That was the end of the conversation that never really got started.

"No problem. Good night." Amp got up and headed for the stairs.

Looking back, he saw Paul sit for a moment in thought before he put his headphones back on.

Amp entered his bedroom and climbed back in bed. After a few minutes, sleep finally took over, but no sooner than he closed his eyes did it seem it was time to start a new day. Something had to give.

"Here you go," Amp said as he came downstairs with a drug-test sample in hand.

Paul took the container. "Any surprises in here?"

"No." Amp shook his head.

Brad came downstairs carrying two large duffle bags. "All right, guys. It's been real, but my ride is here."

"You outta here?" Amp asked.

"Yep," Brad answered happily.

"Where you going?"

"Probably live with my mom for a little while. Just 'til I get on my feet."

"Good luck out there," Amp said.

"You too." Brad then looked to the man who had served as his house manager for the past ninety days. "Later, Paul."

"Later," Paul replied. "And remember what I told you. Don't be an asshole all your life."

Brad smirked.

"Later, Brad," Amp said.

Paul walked away as Amp stood and watched Brad walk out the front door. His time was coming shortly, and seeing Brad released made him even more determined to focus on life outside of this place. His day of freedom couldn't get here fast enough. All the sleepless nights were starting to take a toll on Amp, so he figured he was going to have to go face the ghost that was haunting him. Soon.

Chapter 25

The stage at Club Eden had been transformed into a professional photography studio. A huge backdrop was set up between the pulled-back curtains, and there were two cameras to capture the models from different angles. There were people doing makeup, costumes, stage/prop design, and assistants setting up to make sure everything went smoothly.

Madam was talking with the photographer, bouncing ideas and themes off of him for the calendar shoot, when Dr. Feelgood walked in. All eyes shot toward his direction and stayed glued—not to him, but to what he had in his hand. He stood there with a baby carrier in one hand and a Winnie the Pooh diaper bag hanging on his shoulder.

"Uh-uh. No you don't." Madam stepped away from the photographer and approached Dr. Feelgood. "The sign says twenty-one years of age and older in this club." She looked down at the baby. "He ain't even twenty-one months."

"Come on, Madam," Dr. Feelgood said. "I got a sitter for tonight, but I couldn't find anyone to watch him this afternoon."

"You talk to his momma?"

"Yes, but until we get DNA results, my hands are full." He looked down at the baby. "Literally."

Dr. Feelgood's words were not moving Madam to change her position, not one bit, as she stood there shaking her head. "Doc . . ." she said with that don't-play-with-me tone.

Amp, standing off to the side while one of the female assistants rubbed baby oil on him, spoke up. "Madam, if I may put my two cents in . . ."

Madam gave him a look, advising him to speak at his own risk.

"We do need Doc for the calendar," Amp started, "and we need the calendar to help save the building."

Madam thought about his words for a moment and then gave in." Okay—but do *not* bring that child back here tonight."

Dr. Feelgood exhaled. "Thank you." He looked at Amp and nodded his appreciation.

Dr. Feelgood set the baby down, and Amp teased, "That's a really nice diaper bag," to lighten the tension in the room.

"Shut up!" Dr. Feelgood replied.

They both laughed as everyone finished preparing for the shoot. Within a half hour, it was

"Lights, camera, action!" as the photo shoot began.

It was Madam's idea for each of the guys to shoot individually and then take some shots together. No one tried to outshine the others. This was a group effort with one purpose in mind: to save Club Eden, which meant saving their jobs.

By the time the shoot was a wrap, the photographer had more than enough photos to work with in order to produce the moneymaking calendar. But would it make enough money to help keep the doors open?

Later on that evening, the night's business was just as successful as the photo shoot. Amp and the guys even had to help Madam set up some extra tables and chairs. The club was reaching capacity every night.

Amp had settled up with both Madam and Dime, helped Dime load her car, and was now walking across the parking lot toward home. He was in the middle of the lot when he noticed a black Jaguar parked across the street with the lights on and the engine running.

Amp slowed his pace as a million things went through his mind. The car was parked in front of a vacant building with a FOR SALE sign in the window, so they obviously weren't waiting for someone to come out of the building.

As Amp stepped onto the sidewalk, the car door opened. He could hear his heart pounding.

A few seconds later, Amp felt the tension leave his body as he recognized a familiar face. "This is yours too?" Amp asked Jesse, who was crossing the street to meet up with him.

"Yeah, I got a few of these." He gave Amp some dap then looked over Amp's shoulder at Club Eden. "You know, I didn't believe it when I heard, but I guess my boy Eric was telling the truth. You are up here working." He tilted his head and asked, "You ain't dancing, are you, dude?"

"Yep." Amp shrugged. "I don't have much choice, man." He was no longer ashamed to admit that this was what he'd resorted to in order to make things jump off. At least it was legal.

"Yes, you do have a choice," Jesse said. "I told you that you can come get this money with me. Real money."

"I can't, bruh. Those years I spent locked up, I can't get that back. I ain't doing nothing that can get me sent back. Jay walking, nothing."

Jesse nodded. "Was it really that bad?"

"The things I saw in there . . ." Amp's mind wandered back to his prison days. He had seen men brutalized, raped, murdered, beaten half to death, trampled, stabbed multiple times over the simplest of misunderstandings . . . and that was just the inmates. Some of the corrections officers were just as bad, if not worse than the inmates. They had actually gone as far as setting up beatings and stabbings among rival gang members. As far as Amp was concerned, the warden was a gangster and the corrections officers were the muscle. It was only by the grace of God that Amp made it out of there without experiencing any of the things he'd witnessed happening to others. That place was a special version of hell that Amp would do anything to avoid going back to.

"Yeah, it was really that bad." Amp wasn't trying to stay on memory lane, and besides that, he had curfew. He knew that if they kept talking, Jesse was only going to keep trying to talk him into something illegal.

"Look, I gotta run, bro."

"Yeah, me too. I'll see you around." Jesse walked back over to his car and Amp started walking home.

Jesse drove past him and blew his horn. Amp watched the vehicle, not in envy, but knowing that if he did the right thing, that would be him rolling one day soon. For now, he would focus on helping Madam keep the club so that he'd have a place to make that legit money.

Amp was truly using his black magic to get this particular female to float on cloud nine. It was the middle of his routine, and he'd brought a lovely full-figured woman to the stage. Just as he'd done with the petite school teacher–looking patron, he'd sat this woman in a chair in the middle of the stage and was gyrating around her.

That woman took it all in. Unlike the other girl, she didn't even try to play coy. She wanted everything Amp had to offer, and made it clear by bouncing and throwing right back to Amp what he was giving her.

All of the other women were going crazy over the show Amp and his accomplice were putting on. She became a part of his show, and the two led the voyeurs through a journey of visual ecstasy. Several members of the audience had their mouths open as well as their wallets.

Amp was fulfilling this woman's every fantasy, picking her up and down while showing her and all those watching that he was strong as steel indeed. Then Amp bent the woman over, pulled up her dress, and started grinding on her voluptuous, moist ass.

Amp caught a peep of the floor covered with an abundance of cash, and not just ones either. He made a mental note that if he ever saw this woman in the crowd again, he'd bring her on stage every time.

Once the song ended, Amp helped the woman back to her seat, almost feeling guilty about not sharing his tips with her. She had definitely been the highlight of the show. He knew, though, that the women did not come for the money. They came for the fantasy, and he had given it all to them tonight.

He finished up his routine, collected the money and underwear off the floor, and hit the locker room.

Babyface took the stage next, and as always, he killed his routine.

"Does the baby need breastfeeding, is what I want to know," a woman shouted out during his routine.

At the end of Babyface's routine, the same woman smacked him on his bare butt cheeks as he walked past her in his G-string. When he stopped and turned to her, she said very unapologetically, "When you're ready for your sugar mama, you let me know. You can have anything you want." She winked flirtatiously. The woman looked like money, with her red-bottom shoes and a ring that had to be at least five carats weighing down her finger.

Staying true to his motto, "Never leave money on the table," Babyface walked over to her table and kissed her on the cheek. He inhaled the sexy fragrance sprinkled about her neck. Hell, she even smelled like money. He gladly took the business card she offered him, thinking it may come in handy one day.

Next it was show time for Casanova and El Fuego, and they showed all the way out. Those women couldn't handle Club Eden tonight. El Fuego even worked some fire-throwing into his routine.

All the guys were stepping their game up. If they were going down, then they were going down fighting.

Later on, once the club was cleared of all patrons, Madam, Dime, and all the dancers were gathered in front of the bar.

"All right," Madam said. "Is that everybody?"

"Yep," Babyface answered.

Madam reached into a box on the bar and pulled out a stack of calendars. She handed them to Babyface to pass out.

The calendars were amazing. Amp's picture graced the page for January. He was rocking only a pair of jeans, slung just low enough to show what he was working with. There was something about that V at the bottom of a well-defined stomach that drove women crazy. It was enough to make even the coldest month of the year feel hot, hot, hot!

Babyface, reppin' the month of February, was certainly going to put the women in the mood for love. The way he stretched out across the stage, resting up on his elbow with one leg bent, he was going to have the women wishing they were stretched out next to him, being fed the bowl of cherries beside him.

All the men had done an amazing job, from Dr. Feelgood with his doctor's jacket and nothing underneath for the month of March to Casanova holding the bouquet of flowers in the month of April, and El Fuego setting it off for the month of May, Cinco De Mayo style. The rest of the months were just as hot.

"Make sure everybody gets one," Madam instructed. "I have a box for each of you, and when you run out, I have more."

The guys were too busy looking at the calendar and not really paying much attention to Madam. They were surprised by how well the calendar had turned out. They looked like professional models.

"Listen!" Madam spoke louder to get their undivided attention. "We need to sell all of these, so hit the streets tomorrow. Beauty salons, beauty supply stores, family, friends, whoever. Just sell them. Ten dollars each."

El Fuego held up the calendar, turning it sideways, admiring his own month of May photo. If he had to say so himself, the photos did his fineness complete justice. "We could easily sell this for twenty."

"You're right," Madam agreed. "But we got ten thousand calendars sitting back there, and it's better to sell all of them at ten dollars apiece than to sell half of them for twenty."

"How are we doing so far on raising the money?" Casanova asked. The fellas had been putting in extra work. Hopefully it was paying off.

Madam tightened her lips. "Good, but not good enough, so we need to turn it up. Speaking of which, I need two of you to come in the rest of the week at seven instead of ten. I have private parties and bachelorette parties booked for the rest of the week. Some of you are gonna have to double up."

Dr. Feelgood, El Fuego, and Casanova each raised their hands.

"I'm cool with picking up an extra gig every day," Dr. Feelgood said. "Due to recent developments, I could use the money. Taking care of a baby is expensive."

"Okay. I'll put you on each day," Madam said to Dr. Feelgood. "Alternate with Fuego, Cass, and Face."

"It's a blessing," Casanova said. "Thank you." El Fuego gave Cass the side-eye for his comment but laughed nonetheless.

"Are you going to sell the calendar here on the nights that we work?" Babyface asked.

"You better believe it," Madam said. "We're going to be selling everything: photo opportunities with you guys at the end of each night, towels for the women to wipe you off with, and shirts for you to sign . . . everything." Madam reached into another box and pulled out a stack of papers. "Also, I printed up flyers for the auction. Spread the word while you're out there selling them calendars. We've got a lot to do and a short amount of time to pull this off."

The flyers and calendars were distributed to each of the dancers. Hopefully Casanova was praying and God was listening, Amp thought. All of their livelihoods depended on it.

Chapter 26

Dr. Feelgood, El Fuego, Casanova, Amp, and Babyface all sold the calendars and promoted the upcoming auction at Club Eden by passing out flyers during the day. None of them minded taking time out of their schedules outside of club hours to do so. Madam wasn't just their boss; she had been there for the each of them at one time and in one way or another. Even though Madam wasn't usually all up in her feelings, everyone knew she cared about her dancers, and they all appreciated it.

When her dancers said they'd do whatever they needed to in order to save the club, Madam believed them, and not just because they were worried about losing their jobs. As fine as each of them were and with their faithful customer fan base, they could make money anywhere doing what they did. But they had chosen her, and stuck with her even as things got rough. The loyalty went both ways. They were a family.

Even though Amp hadn't been part of the family for long, he still fit right in, and was just as determined as the others to help save Club Eden. He'd been out with Dime for three hours straight, handing out flyers in the hot Cali sun.

"You been kind of quiet today. You all right?" Dime asked Amp as they pulled up to a red light.

He answered with one syllable: "Yeah."

She turned to look at him. "That's it? Just 'yeah'? What's going on with you, Amp?"

He hesitated for a moment, but then dug out his wallet, pulled a piece of paper from it, and said, "I need a favor. I need you to take me here, please." Amp handed Dime the paper, where he'd written an address. He'd been quiet all day because he was trying to gather his courage to go there and do what he'd been meaning to do for so long. So far, he hadn't been able to bring himself to go, but in this instant, something told him that if he didn't do it now, he might never follow through.

Dime looked down at the address. "You mind if I ask what this is about?"

"Look, you help me do this first; I'll tell you anything you want to know after."

Dime gave him the side-eye.

"I promise," Amp told her. "But we have to do this today, now, before I change my mind." If he talked to Dime about this any further, Amp could just as easily talk himself right out of it. He appreciated her doing this for him and he owed her an explanation, but right now he just wanted to do it before his nerves got the best of him.

Dime looked at the piece of paper, then back at Amp. "Okay." She didn't press.

Twenty minutes later, Dime spotted the address just as she was passing it. She pulled over and parked her car in front of the neighboring house.

"I'll be back," Amp said, opening the car door.

"Who lives here?" Dime asked, looking back over her shoulder at the house.

"I'll tell you everything when I get back," Amp reiterated.

Making his way up the walkway, Amp knocked on the front door of the small, modest-looking but nicely kept house. No one answered for a few seconds, so he raised his fist to knock again. He heard someone call out from the other side of the door.

"Come in."

Amp apprehensively opened the door and walked in, stopping a few feet inside the house. He didn't see anybody around. Clearing his throat, he announced, "I'm looking for Mrs. Patrice Ellis."

A short, happy-looking older woman came bouncing around the corner. She was wearing an apron and drying her hands with a dishtowel, as if she'd been busy in the kitchen. "I'm Patrice Ellis. How can I . . ." Patrice's words trailed off and she froze in her tracks. Her smile was instantly replaced by a look of anger and hurt.

"Mrs. Ellis, I—" Amp couldn't even get his words out before the woman's hand connected sharply with his face, leaving a stinging aftermath on his cheek. Amp's eyes began to water, not because he was in pain. His eyes watered with shame and regret.

"No!" Patrice whispered, horrified.

"Wanted to say I'm sor—" Once again, Patrice stopped his sentence by slapping him. Amp didn't budge.

"No!" she repeated.

"For what happened to Shannon." Amp insisted on getting out what he'd come there to say, and Patrice continued her efforts to slap the words out of Amp's mouth, literally, as once again she hit him, even harder this time. Amp still did not budge, but his tears were flowing freely now. As far as he was concerned, she had every right to inflict pain on him after the turmoil he'd caused in her life. He could see it in her eyes. He could feel her pain. That's why his tears fell: for the hurt he'd caused.

"No. You don't get to apologize!" Patrice said, nothing but rage in her eyes. There were no tears. She'd cried enough over the years. She wasn't about to shed any more due to the actions of the man standing in front of her.

Amp stood there silently. He'd said what he went there to say. There was nothing else that needed to be said, or that Patrice would even allow him to say, for that matter.

He turned to leave, but her voice stopped him in his tracks.

"Wait. You're not getting off that easy. You're going to hear this."

Amp stood facing Patrice. He felt he owed it to her to hear whatever words she had to say to him.

"My daughter was an athlete all her life. The happiest I ever saw her was when she was out on the court or on the track competing. She said sports made her feel alive. Girl could run like the wind. She had a full scholarship to run track at any university of her choice, and you took that away from her when you decided to drink and drive." Patrice had to take a moment to regain her composure. "How much time did you serve? What, four years?"

"Four and a half, ma'am," Amp said quietly.

Patrice shook her head in disapproval of what the courts considered justice. She turned her head to look at Shannon's high school sports pictures, ribbons, and medals, which were hanging in the foyer where they stood. "Four and a half years. What'd she get? Multiple surgeries, two years of rehab on that shattered leg, and a lifetime of dealing with those broken dreams. Sure, she can walk now, thank God. Even jog. But she'll never be the same. And you come in here with 'Sorry.' " The way she glared at Amp . . . if looks could kill.

"Did the judge make you come here?" she asked.

Amp paused for a moment, not sure that she wouldn't slap him if he tried to speak again. "No, ma'am. I wanted to come here," he said after realizing that she was, indeed, waiting for him to reply.

"For what?"

"To apologize. I'm out of jail and I'm working now. And because I was the reason she lost her scholarship, I wanted to help pay for some of her college classes."

Patrice looked down, then looked at her daughter's pictures on the wall. Amp looked at them as well. He knew no amount of money could change the heartache he'd caused her family. "Is the court making you do this as part of some restitution or something?" she asked.

Amp shook his head. "No, ma'am."

Patrice said nothing for a while, but the lines of anger on her forehead softened a little. Amp was hopeful that she was actually considering his offer. Finally she said, "I need to talk this over with Shannon. It's her decision."

She turned around and went to a small writing desk, where she retrieved a piece of paper and a pen. Handing it to Amp, she said, "Write down your number. One of us will contact you."

Amp wrote his information, handed it to her, and then left. He exhaled upon hitting the fresh air. For so long he'd been suffocated by those words trapped in his mind, weighed down with so much guilt, shame, and regret. Although he knew it didn't compare to the pain, loss, and hurt the Ellises had gone through and would have to deal with for the rest of their lives, it was difficult for him nonetheless.

The hardest part was now over. He'd said the words "I'm sorry." It was over, but now, as he walked to the car, he realized that he'd have to relive it just one more time as he kept his promise to Dime and told her everything.

Chapter 27

Amp got inside Dime's car, closed the door, and sat back looking straight ahead. He was still visibly shaken from his episode with Patrice, and his face was still stinging. He rubbed his cheek and opened and closed his mouth a couple times, making sure his jawbone wasn't out of whack or anything due to the triple blow he'd received.

"Are you okay?" Dime asked. The keys were in the ignition, but the car wasn't running.

"You drive; I'll talk," Amp replied. He knew it would be easier to tell the story if she was focused on the road and not peering at him.

Dime drove past several houses before Amp started to talk.

"About five years ago, I was at a party one night. I had a couple drinks."

Amp had barely started telling his story, and the anguish could already be heard in his voice.

"I wasn't drunk," he continued, "but I was definitely buzzed. After the party was over, I thought

I was okay to drive home. Biggest mistake of my life." Amp paused for a moment, and Dime remained silent, allowing him to continue. "I was coming up on this light as it turned yellow. I thought I could make it, so instead of slowing down, I sped up and went faster. I ended up running the red light and broadsiding this car."

Inside Amp's head, he could see the nightmare that had been so vividly haunting him in his sleep. He could see his hands gripping the steering wheel. He could feel the fracture of his ankle after slamming down on and holding the brakes for dear life. He could hear the crashing sound of the cars colliding. He could taste the blood on his tongue. He could smell the burnt rubber and the smoke coming from under the hood of his car.

"The whole driver's side door was caved in. They had to cut the driver out of the car." Amp put his head down and swallowed.

"Did the driver die?" Dime asked hesitantly.

"She lived, but her leg was broken up really bad. They thought she might not walk again. I spent six months in jail waiting on a trial. They gave me four more years in prison. It would have been more, but it was my first offense."

Dime kept her eyes on the road. If she was stunned by what Amp was telling her, she did not show it on her face. "So that's why you don't drink?"

"Yep."

"You could have told me."

"I thought that when you found out what I'd done, you wouldn't want anything to do with me."

She shook her head and told him, "You are not the sum of all your mistakes. You can't let that define you. Besides, who am I to judge you? We all got our shit."

Amp looked over at Dime, wondering what story she was carrying inside her. *We all got our shit.* She sounded like Paul.

"Yeah, we sure do," he said sincerely.

Dime pointed upward. "If He can forgive you, then you can forgive you."

Amp gave her a small, thankful smile.

Later on that night, Club Eden was lit up from the outside, buzzing with patrons walking into the club and cars pulling into the practically filled parking lot. The music could be heard outside as the new security guard, who had replaced Amp, checked IDs at the door.

Inside the club it was loud, and the women were full of energy and having a good time as

Dr. Feelgood started his show. Casanova walked by with two women, on his way to give them a private dance since he'd just finished his set. Madam was selling shirts, hats, stickers, towels, calendars, and more.

El Fuego hit the stage next and killed it as usual, so much so that women were lined up with calendars for him to autograph. Babyface showed out when he brought not one, not two, but three women on stage during his routine and still managed to make each one feel as if she were the only one there.

It was an epic night for the club; hopefully it would be successful enough to put a huge dent in the money Madam owed. Otherwise, it might be the last epic night for the club ever.

Amp waved good-bye to Dime after she'd dropped him off, and he went inside the house. It was almost three in the morning, and Paul was sitting in a chair with his records and headphones, as usual. Amp decided not to even bother intruding on his moment this time.

"Second degree murder."

Amp stopped in his tracks when he heard Paul speak.

"That's what I did time for."

Amp walked over and sat across from Paul without saying a word. Paul took off the headphones and put them around his neck with the music still playing.

"I was twelve years old," Paul said. "Wanted to be in this gang so bad. Wanted to belong to something. They jumped me in. Beat my ass. Then I had to prove myself. The gang that we were beefing with had just shot up half our neighborhood. So, one night we went driving through their neighborhood. We came across a group of them."

Amp just listened. He was reaping what he had sown. He'd finally decided to share his story with Dime; now Paul had decided to open up and do the same with him. It made Amp feel good that Paul thought enough of him to open up like this.

"They gave me a gun and told me to start shooting. I did. I closed my eyes and pulled the trigger three times. It was just supposed to scare them.

"First two shots didn't hit anything. Third shot . . . hit a boy my age in the head. He died immediately. Soon as the police came around asking questions, the same gang that was supposed to be my new family blamed it all on me. Threatened my life if I said anything, and turned their backs on me.

"I wasn't an adult, so they couldn't give me life. I spent age twelve to eighteen in juvenile detention. At eighteen, they moved me to prison, where I spent the next fifteen years.

"When I got out five years ago, my parole officer wasn't an asshole like Mr. Barrett, but really wanted to keep us cats out of jail and off the streets. He told me they were looking to train someone to do this job. Said they wanted someone that knew how to interact with felons. Who better than a convict? So, he hooked up the interview, I was offered the job, I took it, and here I am."

He adjusted the headphones as if he was getting ready to put them back over his ears.

"You know you can't hide out in here forever, man," Amp said before Paul could put them on. "You still got a lot of life left to live, if you want it. You could be out there making sure other kids don't make the same mistake you did. Catch them before they get into the system. Get your degree and teach or something."

Paul just stared at him, so Amp kept talking.

"I'm gonna say this; then I'm gonna shut up."

"Good," Paul said.

"You got a second chance just like I did. I'm gonna do something with my second chance."

Amp got up and walked upstairs, leaving Paul sitting there in thought.

The next morning, Amp was in the kitchen scarfing down his breakfast when Paul came in.

"Where you off to this morning?" Paul asked him, as if last night's talk had never happened.

"Run some errands and then going to put a deposit down on my apartment." With Paul's help, Amp had found a small one-bedroom apartment just north of the 10 freeway. It was about ten minutes from the halfway house, so he'd still be close to his job as well. "I'm out of here in a week."

Amp had been averaging almost two thousand dollars a week since he'd started dancing at the club two months ago. He had just over fifteen thousand saved up between the bank account Dime had taken him to open up and the money he'd already stored in the safe at the halfway house. One could say he had placed his eggs in more than one basket.

"You know, it does me good to see one of you come through here and really do something with this opportunity," Paul said.

"I wouldn't have had it if you hadn't approved me for it." Amp began to gather up his dirty dishes. "I'll be back after work."

Paul headed into the other room as Amp placed his dirty dishes in the sink. Before he could get out the door, his cell phone rang. He pulled it out and answered without checking the caller ID.

"Hello." As Amp listened to the caller, his expression became solemn. "Thank you," he said then ended the call and hurried out the door to catch the bus.

An hour later, Amp found himself cautiously walking back up to the same house that Dime had taken him to the other day. He could see a young woman, maybe a year or two younger than him, sitting on the porch. She had that same natural beauty like Dime, only she had that girl-next-door type of thing going on. When she saw Amp, she stood.

"Hi," Amp greeted as he walked up on the porch.

"Hello," she replied. "Amp?"

He nodded. Amp recognized the girl from the picture in the newspaper article that he kept near his bed. At long last, right in front of him stood Shannon, the daughter of Patrice Ellis and the victim of his drunk driving accident.

"Thank you for seeing me." Amp looked at the front door nervously.

"My mother's not here," Shannon said. "After hearing her replay of what had taken place between you and her, I figured you would be a little leery about coming back over and risking an ambush."

"It's fine. I had it coming," he said, even though relief at Patrice's absence was written across his face. Amp held his breath for a second, then blurted out, "I wanted to tell you that I'm sorry for what I did to you. I think about it every day. I always will."

Shannon was silent for a moment; then she nodded. "I forgive you."

Her words caught Amp off guard. After the way her mother had acted, he'd expected much of the same from Shannon. "How? I mean, why?" he asked quietly. Forgiveness seemed to have come so easy. He wanted it, but in the back of his mind, he wondered whether he really deserved it. He hadn't forgiven himself.

"I had to. Couldn't keep dragging that anger and resentment around. I prayed for you, and then I let it go."

Amp was speechless.

"My mother told me about your offer to help me pay for school. If I needed it, I would accept it, but I'm on a full academic scholarship, so as long as I stay on these books, it's all taken care of." She looked in Amp's eyes. "You know, it took a lot of guts for you to come here like you did. I appreciate that."

"Took even more guts for you to forgive me—so thank you."

Shannon gave Amp a small smile and a nod. Sensing that there was nothing more to be said between them, Amp nodded back, waved, and then walked away.

He couldn't help but notice that something felt different. It was as if he were a hundred pounds lighter. The weight of the guilt, shame, and regret that he had become accustomed to carrying was gone. This was a new start indeed, and although he'd never forget the consequences of his actions that night, he expected far fewer sleepless nights.

Chapter 28

The last few patrons were leaving Club Eden one night as Amp walked up to Madam. She'd been sitting alone at one of the tables.

"So how are you holding up?" Amp asked, pulling out a chair and joining her.

"I'm making it." She sighed and then looked around the club. "I am glad I decided to fight for this place. At least that way, if I lose it—"

"Which you won't," Amp interrupted. "Madam, you can't say stuff like that. You can't speak doubt and negativity and expect good things to happen."

Madam didn't have a comeback because Amp was right. "I'm supposed to be the one teaching you guys about life."

"You are." Amp stood, resting a supportive hand on Madam's shoulder, and then walked over to the bar where the other dancers were gathered.

Amp crossed paths with Casanova, who walked over to Madam and handed her an envelope. Madam left to go into her office, and Casanova joined the others at the bar.

"I can't believe we sold all those calendars," he said in disbelief. He and El Fuego had paired up and covered the Latin and suburban neighborhoods, while the others hit the hood to sell every last box of calendars.

"I can't believe you, of all people, sold the most," El Fuego said.

"Church women are the freakiest," Casanova replied, and they all shared a laugh. "Sorry, Lord," he said, looking upward.

Dr. Feelgood, who had been walking around on cloud nine all night, walked behind the bar and poured everybody a shot. "All right, everybody grab one. Amp, yours is the juice." He pushed Amp's glass toward him.

Amp nodded and smiled.

"I got some good news," Dr. Feelgood said, holding up his glass. "The test came back today."

Judging from his good mood, all the guys were expecting to hear a "not-guilty" verdict.

"He's mine. I'm officially a father." He cracked a big smile, and everyone raised their glasses to congratulate him.

"Congratulations, man, but uh, we all kind of knew that already. You see the nose on that boy," Amp said with a laugh.

Dr. Feelgood flinched.

"Aw, come on. I'm kidding, man. That's a handsome little guy you've got. Congrats. Way to man up and handle your business."

Amp and Dr. Feelgood dapped then downed their drinks.

"So how's the mother taking it?" Babyface asked.

"Fine, actually," Dr. Feelgood said. "She ain't pressing me to get back together. Just wants me there for my boy. We even figured out a new arrangement. I keep him on the three days that I don't work here. She has him the rest of the week, and I help her with anything she needs for him."

"You're lucky," Babyface said. "It isn't always that peaceful."

"I know," Dr. Feelgood replied.

Madam came out of her office and walked back over to the bar. All of the guys quieted down.

"I just really wanted to thank you guys," Madam said. "The money from the extra shows you've been doing and from the calendars has made a nice dent in the amount I have to turn in on Monday. I didn't want to, but I sold one of my cars to help us get closer to the mark. The good news is, if we bring in twenty thousand in the auction tomorrow, we should have enough to keep the club open."

Amp smiled on the outside, but he had a dilemma on the inside. He'd told himself that if need be, he'd dip into his own pockets to help save the club, but that was before he'd gotten used to the idea of having saved up about sixteen grand. That money was a guaranteed ticket toward starting over in life on a comfortable note. The more he had built his savings, the less he had even thought about getting into something illegal to make extra ends. Hopefully everything would work out as planned and the cash flow for Madam would come in, but he'd just have to cross that bridge when he got to it.

The guys looked relieved that Madam had come up with as much money as she had, but seeing the finish line wasn't the same as actually crossing it. Anything could happen in the meantime.

"So, I want you to get some rest tonight, and I want you suited and booted tomorrow. Auction starts at eight; be here by six. Sharp. Now get out of here." Madam pointed to the exit and then went back into her office.

The next evening at six, they returned to the club with garment bags in hand. Madam had been there since early afternoon preparing for that night's auction.

"Come on in, guys," Madam said, escorting them into the locker room with urgency. There was a well-dressed, dark-skinned gentleman waiting in there. "I know originally I had told you guys I just wanted you to wear your best suits. Well, you can hang them up over there." She pointed toward the clothing rack. "There has been a slight change of plans. My friend David Frere, designer of Musika Frere, is going to get you guys dressed more appropriately for the evening."

Having no idea what Madam had up her sleeve, the guys filed over to the rack, hung up their suits, and waited on David to do what he needed to do. Madam exited the locker room, leaving David to do his thing. David and his seamstress immediately began sizing them up, and the fitting process began.

After working his magic, the head of the two-man glam squad went to Madam's office and peeped his head in. "Madam Fox, can you come out here for a second?" David walked back to the stage area where the guys were waiting.

Madam walked out of her office and stopped in her tracks, admiring the sight before her. "Now that's what the hell I'm talking about," she whooped.

The guys were all lined up shoulder to shoulder, wearing finely tailored traditional black tuxedos and bowties. Casanova looked like he could be the next James Bond, as his aura screamed sophistication. Dr. Feelgood looked like the black James Bond. El Fuego's tux fit incredibly well and complemented his Latin features. Babyface was on point. He looked like money, signifying what they hoped to bring in lots of tonight. Amp was now a far cry from door security. He looked so classic, like a young Denzel. Each dancer looked like a million bucks, and if everything went as planned, they would definitely make the big bucks. This was the last opportunity to save Club Eden . . . legally.

Chapter 29

Amp noticed Dime walking into Club Eden carrying some of her equipment. She was making a beeline straight to her booth, until she looked toward the stage and had to do a double take. Keeping her eyes glued on the sight before her, she placed the equipment down on one of the tables in slow motion.

She walked over and stood next to Madam. "Damn . . ." she said, admiring the men in their tuxedos. One by one, Dime allowed her eyes to view each man as if she were trying to pick someone out of a police lineup.

"Girl, that's what I said," Madam told her.

Dime walked past each dancer, eyeing him up and down. "All right then."

Madam looked at her watch and then clapped her hands together. "Here we go. Oh, and fellas, you better grab a Red Bull or 5-hour ENERGY. If these women are spending a few grand on you for the evening, you might need it."

Several groups of women had bought tables for the night's auction. The women at the table with the highest bid would have the pleasure of being entertained by the dancer they purchased for the remainder of the evening. The dancer, of course, could give dances, with the dances getting as sexy as the purchaser would like. He could give the women massages, or just talk and have drinks with them. He could give them the most amazing and personal VIP lap dance ever. The women could even choose to have him sit back while they gave him a dance—any kind they wanted, including a strip tease if they were bold enough.

Touching was not prohibited, by either party, as long as the women were down for it. That meant they could touch the dancer's body, rub oil on him, slap his ass, whatever money could buy. Almost anything was okay. The only rule was that there was absolutely no sex.

"These women are expecting the time of their lives," Madam said. "Packed into four hours."

The guys looked at each other with matching expressions: *Oh, shit.*

A half hour later, the parking lot was packed and cars were still pulling in, some eventually having to park on the street as the lot reached capacity. Groups of women entered the building, excited and ready to party. Tonight they were going to get the opportunity that each one had hoped for every night: that she'd be the one to get all of a dancer's attention. Well, that fantasy would be fulfilled, if the price was right.

The crew Madam had hired to decorate the place had adorned each round table with a white linen tablecloth. There was a single rose in a vase on each table, and some loose rose petals scattered about. Each place setting had a wine glass as part of tonight's bottomless wine glass special. It was the servers' job to make sure they kept the all-you-can-drink wine flowing. An assortment of crab cakes, wings, calamari, and other starters was on each table as well. Each chair had a small circular fan with a number on it that the women could use for bidding.

There were several VIP tables, which had been purchased by a group of women who wanted to sit together. Those tables each had a large circular fan in the middle for the representative that would be bidding on behalf of the entire table. Use of that particular fan signified that the table was bidding collectively. In other words, these chicks meant business.

The lights in the room were dimmed, coupled with grown and sexy music. It made for a perfect atmosphere for all that was about to take place this evening.

Every person had paid twenty-five dollars to get in, and there were at least three hundred women packing Club Eden at ten to a table. The VIP tables to the front had been purchased for $500 each. The rest of the tables, which were just a little further back, were where the smaller groups or individuals sat.

The dancers were walking around, mingling in the crowd and buttering up the women to get them to go deep into their pockets. It was also a form of meet and greet, allowing the women to get an idea of exactly who they wanted to bid on.

Amp was getting his mingle on, but out of habit, he kept an eye on everything and everyone.

Madam was over at the bar talking to a few of the servers. She'd hired extra help to assist with the big night. The servers who were tending to the tables were all attractive men. Of course Madam had to give her clientele an appetizer before the main course was served, so each server was athletic, muscular, and just plain hot. They were wearing black slacks and bowties with no shirts. They were exactly what was needed to get the women all heated up before the bidding began.

"I see too many empty glasses out here." She scanned the room. "Keep those glasses full and make sure everyone is having a great time, so they'll be ready to spend when it's time for the auction."

The servers hurried back to work, and the wine began to flow. This made sense to Amp as well, so he grabbed a bottle and started pouring wine for some of the guests. The other dancers followed suit, and Madam nodded to Amp with approval.

The sound of laughter, good music, and great stories of what each woman desired from her man if she was the lucky bidder filled the air as the club reached capacity. The time for the auction was now approaching. Madam signaled for each dancer to make his way to the stage. With all of the men lined up shoulder to shoulder behind her, she stepped in front of the mic, ready to kick things off.

"Can I have everyone's attention, please?" Madam announced. "Before we start, I just want to remind everyone of the rules. Number one: the most money gets the guy. Two: you can have the gentleman you buy dance, rub your shoulders, massage your feet, play in your hair; whatever you, your dancer, and your group agree on. We also have party rooms in the back if your group wants a little privacy."

There were several *ooh*s and *ahh*s from the crowd. A couple of women even high-fived one another, agreeing that that was indeed part of the plan.

"Three: when bidding, please use the circular number that is on your table. And lastly, cash only. If there are no questions, let's begin."

The women applauded in excitement and anticipation.

The guys all went backstage, and the house lights were dimmed. A few seconds later, Casanova stepped out into the spotlight on the stage. A huge picture of a shirtless Casanova appeared on the screen that was set up behind him.

"I present to you," Madam said from off to the side, "Casanova!"

The applause grew louder. Dime started the music.

"The bidding shall commence at one thousand dollars."

Three different tables of women started bidding. The fans were flying up all over the place at those three tables. It was clear that the women had decided in advance who they just had to have. Some of them were truly pissed off when the bidding got too high for them to afford and they had to drop out.

"Sold for three thousand dollars!" Madam announced after the final bid was placed. She walked over to the table, collected the money, and signaled Casanova over to the table of overly excited women, the first winners of the night.

Casanova kept a smile on his face as he walked over to the table, but under his breath he mumbled, "Jesus, take the wheel."

Madam returned to the front of the room and introduced El Fuego as his picture appeared on the screen behind him. Dime started the music, and the excitement and bidding began between four different tables: two groups of Latino women, a group of white women, and a group of black women. The bidding went back and forth many times, the Latinas of all shades and builds bound and determined to show love for their own. Eventually one of the groups of Latino women prevailed, outbidding the other three tables.

"Sold for five thousand dollars!" Madam was more than pleased to announce. She was working that room, handling her business as she walked over to the table and collected the money. She signaled El Fuego to the table, where he gladly went to spend the evening with his native sisters.

Madam returned to the front of the room and introduced Babyface. His shirtless and sexy picture popped up on the big screen, and the bidding began. One woman sat alone at a table in the back, and she was determined not to lose. She was rocking a fly black hat with a mean lean to it, her hair slicked back in a ponytail, and she was wearing dark Dior shades. She never put her bidding fan down, outbidding everyone after several rounds back and forth.

"Sold for seven thousand dollars!" Madam announced, making her way over to the table to collect. Madam signaled for Babyface to follow her. The woman who had been doing the bidding set the bundle of money on the table and took off her sunglasses.

Babyface's mouth dropped when the woman's face was revealed. It was Valerie, the woman who had destroyed his car in the parking lot. Madam looked stunned, but Babyface, on the other hand, was pleasantly surprised.

"They can't have my man," Valerie said pointedly. She stood up, picked up the money from the table, and put it in Madam's hand. "And you've got some making up to do," Valerie said to Babyface.

Babyface stepped around Madam to Valerie, put his hand around the back of her neck, paused for a second, and then pulled her in for a kiss.

Madam walked back to the front of the room with a smile. Babyface could deal with Valerie if he wanted to. She'd paid for him, so now he was all hers anyway.

Next Madam introduced Dr. Feelgood, and he stepped out into the spotlight. Women could be heard tallying how much money they had in their groups. This time the bidding began between five tables, and it went on for a while. When it seemed like the bidding was slowing down, Dr. Feelgood started to undo his belt a little, and the bidding became feverish again. Eventually, one group of women placed a bid that no one could beat.

"Sold for ten thousand dollars!" Madam was beside herself. She walked over to collect the money, and then he went to greet his high-rolling fans.

Madam headed back to the front of the room. "Last but not least," she announced, "Black Magic!"

Amp walked out into the spotlight, and the energy started to build. There were five tables bidding on Amp. It was serious now. He was the last dancer, so a lot was at stake with these women. Two of the tables that hadn't won a bid yet didn't want to risk ending the night without a man, so they pushed their tables together and agreed to team up and pool their money together. They eventually outbid the other groups.

"Sold for fifteen thousand dollars." Madam had done the math in her head and knew at that moment that they had more than enough money to pay the debt to keep Club Eden open.

She walked over to the table, collected and counted the money, then signaled to Amp to come to the table that had moments ago been two separate tables. Amp had his work cut out for him with all these women. He took a deep breath, then headed over to the table, drinking a 5-hour ENERGY on the way over. If Casanova wasn't already busy with a group of women himself, Amp might have asked him to pray for him. The way these women were eyeing Amp and licking their lips as he walked over to the table, it looked as though they were prepared to eat him alive.

Madam went to the front of the room and grabbed the microphone one last time. "All right, ladies. Enjoy your purchases." She looked to Dime. "You know what to do."

Dime faded out the grown and sexy music and let the strip club music fly. Immediately, the energy in the building doubled. Some of the guys started dancing for their groups, others started massaging the shoulders and feet of their purchasers. El Fuego was laid out across the table wearing only his thong while the group of women that won the bid ate fruit and chocolate off his body. All of this and the night was still young. No telling what was yet to come.

Chapter 30

It had been a long night at Club Eden, but a successful one, so no one was complaining, not even over the fact that the club had stayed open a few minutes past usual closing hours. After all the thousands of dollars those women had paid to spend time with the dancers, there would have been a riot up in that place had anyone even tried to ask them to leave.

Madam had to signal Dime to cut the music off. Of course, no more alcohol could be served, so eventually, with no music playing and no liquid courage flowing, the women got the hint and began to file out.

Dime was getting all of her equipment together. The guys were back in their regular clothes, talking and laughing as they finished picking up the place. Madam came out of her office trying to hide the huge smile on her face. Her hands were behind her back.

She stood in the middle of the club, looking like she had the biggest secret and she would explode if she didn't tell it.

"I have to thank you all," Madam said. She was so overcome with joy that she had to pause. Swallowing the tears that threatened to start, she told them proudly, "Monday morning, I will personally drop off a check for the total amount of those back taxes, and we are free and clear."

Everyone cheered, dapped, and high-fived one another. Amp was elated. He had been so busy entertaining the women all night that he hadn't kept count of the dollars Madam was taking in from the auction. He knew the patrons were spending wildly, so he knew they would at least come close, but close wasn't good enough when it came to paying the government. Truth be told, he'd been prepared to offer his personal funds if he had to, but now he was relieved to know that he wouldn't have to cough up a large chunk of his hard-earned money to help keep the club open.

"On top of that, we made eighteen thousand more than we needed," Madam continued, "so I figured a two thousand dollar thank you to each of you should cover it. That sound about right?" She whipped the envelopes full of money from behind her back.

Now that was an added bonus the men hadn't seen coming but very much appreciated. Amp was especially grateful, considering he was about to be paying rent and furnishing an apartment.

Casanova was looking up and counting on his fingers when he said, "Actually, eighteen thousand divided by—"

"Cass!" Amp cut him off.

"I was just playing." Casanova laughed.

Madam shot Cass a look and pretended to try to take his envelope back. Everyone's mood was jubilant as they celebrated the victory brought about by their hard work.

Just as Madam had turned to head back into her office, a voice stopped her.

"So maybe I don't know how to bow out gracefully after all."

She couldn't even fight off the huge grin that spread across her face. She turned around only to be standing mere feet from the man who had a grip on her heart.

Madam slowly walked over to Marcus until they were nose to nose. "Maybe that just means the show isn't really over," she said in a whisper.

"Or maybe we just need an encore," Marcus said in a deep, succulent voice.

"Maybe," Madam agreed with Marcus.

Amp raised an eyebrow. This was the first time he had seen her be vulnerable and let her guard down for a man. She had taught him so much about life and business, but in this moment, she was teaching him how to let go and love. He definitely made a mental note and quietly exited the room with the other fellas so these two reunited love birds could have time alone.

Amp only had about ten minutes before curfew. Even though this was his last night at the halfway house before moving into his apartment in the morning, he didn't want to disrespect Paul's rules by coming in after three. With it being so close to curfew, he gladly accepted a ride home from Dime.

The next morning, Amp was almost finished packing up his duffle bag. Paul came to his bedroom door.

"It's the big day. You ready?" Paul asked.

"Yes," Amp replied. He looked around the room. "When I first got here, I was afraid I was going to mess up again." Amp had to admit that he'd been tempted several times to talk to Jesse and get put on. Now he was proud of himself for not going that route. Fast, easy money could have definitely led to slow, hard time. He looked at Paul. "I'm not anymore."

"That's good to hear."

"What about you? You ever gonna get outta here and live a little bit?"

Paul thought for a second and shrugged. "Yeah." He cracked a slight smile. "Why not?"

Amp nodded, glad to hear Paul wasn't going to spend the rest of his days closed up in that halfway house with headphones on, listening to blues records. He chuckled inside at that thought.

"Thank you for everything," Amp told Paul.

Amp zipped up his duffle bag and headed out of the room. Paul saw the shoebox with old pictures and newspaper clippings in it in the corner of the room.

"You forgot a box," Paul said.

Amp stopped and looked back at the shoebox. "No, I didn't. I'm not dragging that stuff around with me anymore. This is a new start. I'm going to make some new memories. Take some new pictures." He turned to leave. "I'll be in touch."

Amp walked out of the room, down the stairs, and out the door, where Dime was waiting for him in the driveway. Amp put his bags in the trunk of Dime's car and slammed it closed, then walked over to Dime, who was leaning against the car with a smile on her face. Amp grabbed her arm and pulled her close. Reaching up to hold her face, Amp looked deep into her eyes. Their lips were almost touching. They had both wanted this for way too long.

Then, it happened. Amp pressed his lips softly against hers. She exhaled as he breathed in her kiss. It was the sweetest kiss he'd ever had, the best thing he had ever tasted, and for just a second, the earth stopped spinning.

Amp slowly pulled away, remembering that they were in front of the halfway house and knowing that there would be thousands of those to come.

Slightly dazed, Dime shook it off and they got in the car.

"All set?" Dime asked as she shifted the gear into reverse.

Amp nodded, still staring at the bedroom window. "Yep."

Dime backed out of the driveway and drove away.

Just like when he left the prison, Amp was tempted to look back. *Maybe a quick peek in the rearview mirror*, he thought but then decided against it. He remembered something that old convict Martell had told him in prison:

"You ever wonder why the rearview mirror in a car is so much smaller than the front windshield?" Martell had asked Amp.

"No, I never thought about it."

"It's because the things behind you, the things you've already made it through, are nowhere near as important as the things that lay ahead. Stop looking back and live, young blood."

Those had been some of the realest words Amp had ever heard. Martell was right. It was time to let the past go and start building a new future. *Who knows*, Amp thought while looking at Dime out of the corner of his eye. *She may be a part of that future.*

"Thanks again," Amp said to Dime.

"Don't thank me. You're gonna work this off."

Amp turned to her, looking confused. "What?"

"Yep. Gas money, a lap dance . . . something."

"Okay. You better stop and get some money. I don't work for singles. I have standards."

Dime smiled. "Okay, Mr. Standards. And I meant to ask, how you gonna call yourself *Black Magic* and you're beige?"

Amp looked down at his arms. They both burst out laughing as she drove Amp down the street toward the start of his new life.

The End . . . or the Beginning?

Author's Note

I was born in Detroit, Michigan and grew up right up the expressway, in Flint. I was in and out of foster care homes and group homes from ages four to eighteen. It was during those years that a love for writing was born.

It started initially with songs and poetry. Not wanting to be teased about these writings, I kept quiet about them for the first few years. Around the time I hit college, I had amassed dozens of stories, songs, and poems, and now I wasn't afraid to share them with the world.

In 2005, I wrote my first complete screenplay. It was called *The Timberland Diary*. I ended up having to change the name, so the film was called *Note to Self*. After many rejections, I found Tri Destined Studios, and they gave me a yes. We teamed up with two other studios to make the film. It turned out amazing. I have written ten more films and various TV shows since then.

I thank you for supporting my endeavor by purchasing and reading *Ladies Night*. It is the first novel I have ever written, but there will be more. Many more . . .

Oh, and get ready for the *Ladies Night* movie coming soon!